When I think about that

was wrong. But I didn't

I can feel some kind of sadness that was there with us, but I just wasn't aware of it. I knew something was wrong. I knew there was something different about Dad. It was like he was almost haunted by something, and that made him drive faster and drink even more.

But I never would have asked him about it. That was never the way he and I were together. We talked about my problems and we talked about life and politics and sports and we joked and laughed. But we never talked about anything that might be bothering Dad, because he wasn't that kind of person. He was the kind of person who could handle anything, who could make everything all right.

So that's why I just sat there and watched the billboards and freeway signs flash into view and then disappear. I was staring straight ahead, daydreaming, and even though we were back in the city, I still thought the horizon stretched on forever.

ALSO AVAILABLE IN LAUREL-LEAF BOOKS:

BREAKING BOXES, *A. M. Jenkins*
THE KILLER'S COUSIN, *Nancy Werlin*
FOR MIKE, *Shelley Sykes*
HOLES, *Louis Sachar*
FOR THE LOVE OF VENICE, *Donna Jo Napoli*
HATE YOU, *Graham McNamee*
CLOSE TO A KILLER, *Marsha Qualey*
TIME ENOUGH FOR DRUMS, *Ann Rinaldi*
ANNA OF BYZANTIUM, *Tracy Barrett*
NOBODY ELSE HAS TO KNOW, *Ingrid Tomey*

CONDITIONS of LOVE

Ruth Pennebaker

Special thanks go to my daughter, Teal, and her friends Jessica Light, Lisa Zhang, and Amy Zentmeyer for their patience in educating me about their lives at a high school that also served cappuccino.

Published by
Dell Laurel-Leaf
an imprint of
Random House Children's Books
a division of Random House, Inc.
1540 Broadway
New York, New York 10036

ISBN: 0-440-22834-4

RL: 5.8

Reprinted by arrangement with Henry Holt and Company, Inc.

Printed in the United States of America

December 2000

10 9 8 7 6 5 4 3 2 1

OPM

For Nicholas

CONDITIONS of LOVE

one

If you came to visit our high school, I bet you'd never notice me. That's because I'm a very ordinary person. You'd notice all the girls who are tall and thin and blond and beautiful.

After school, you can see those girls with their boyfriends. The boys put their arms around their girlfriends' shoulders, like they're afraid the girls are going to float away if they don't hold on to them. Sometimes they stop behind a tree and kiss. I try not to stare when they do that, but I can't help it. I've never been kissed, and I think I could use some pointers. In our health class, they told us all about embryos and sperm and menstruation, but they never said anything about kissing. That's why sex education is such a big failure. Do you know what I mean? They never tell you important details like how wide you should open your mouth when you get kissed.

If you came to our high school, you'd also notice that they serve cappuccino in the cafeteria. People who don't go to our school joke about the cappuccino like it's very symbolic of our lives. *They serve cappuccino at Hillside Park High School,* they say, and then they roll their eyes. They also roll their eyes when they talk about all the BMWs and Land Rovers and Lexuses in our student parking lot. *If you see an old, beat-up car, it probably belongs to one of their teachers,* they say.

Everyone says that Hillside Park is one of the best public schools in the country. That's because the students make high scores on standardized tests and they all go to college after they graduate. I think they probably send you to an insane asylum or to the marines if you don't do well on all the standardized tests. I'm taking a journalism class, and I may do an exposé about that. I think a lot of things about this school need to be exposed right now. I probably won't do it, though. If you're going to do an investigative report, you should be very tough and you shouldn't get your feelings hurt all the time, the way I do. That's why I'm not going to be a journalist when I grow up. I'm thinking about being a veterinarian instead.

Nana, my grandmother, says I should feel lucky to go to a school like this, since it's so good academically and it's so safe. I guess she's right. From the outside, Hillside Park looks kind of like a redbrick country club, and there aren't any metal detectors or security guards at the doors. No one carries weapons, unless you count Ashley Skiles's fingernails, which are about three feet long. One time I heard a teacher say that Ashley's fingernails were a lot sharper than her mind.

But sometimes I think Nana is wrong. Sometimes I don't feel lucky to go to school here. Lots of times, I feel like a big failure. Everybody seems happy and beautiful and popular here, except for me and my best friend, Ellie Peterson. Neither of us has ever had a date. If I get hit by a Suburban tomorrow, then I could die without ever having a boyfriend. That would be tragic, kind of like *Romeo and Juliet*, but without Romeo. I wonder what they'd say about me in the student newspaper if that happened. *Freshman Girl Slaughtered in Front of HPHS!*—that would make a nice headline. Even if I'm not going to be a journalist, I spend a lot of my time making up headlines and subheads. *Only Friend Says She Had Very Low Self-Esteem*—maybe that's what they'd use as a subhead. It might make lots of people feel guilty.

Sometimes I think I should join a gang so I'd have more friends. Last year somebody started a rumor that HPHS had a girls' gang called the Chihuahuas. Then someone else said you had to kill a cat as an initiation rite to get in the gang. It was exciting because all the parents and teachers went totally bonkers.

They held lots of meetings about protecting their cats and keeping gangs in the inner-city schools, where they belong. Amy Westner's mom got up and said that girls' gangs were exactly what happened when you stopped encouraging your daughters toward healthy, Christian pursuits like cheerleading and drill teams. I heard that Amy's mother started crying while she was at the podium. She said that these days no one appreciates how you can be a member of a drill team and still retain your individuality.

But after all of that, nothing happened. Not a thing. Zero, zip, nada. The rumors stopped, and no one heard anything more about the Chihuahuas. No one saw any dead cats, either, except a few that got squashed in the middle of the street. The whole thing was very disappointing. Coach Morrison, who teaches world history when he's not yelling at the football team, says that shows how a strong community can fight off youth violence.

You have to fight for peace. That's what Coach Morrison always says. In fact, he's saying it right now. He's pacing in front of our first-period class, and he has chalk-dust marks all over his khaki pants. He's waving his arms in the air and he looks excited, like the team just scored a touchdown. I haven't been paying attention, as usual, so I don't know who he's talking about. The Romans, maybe. The trouble is, the way Coach Morrison teaches history, every era sounds exactly alike.

All of a sudden, he stops pacing. He stands up taller and crosses his arms and looks straight ahead. That's what he always does when he's telling us something he thinks is important. Everyone pays attention then, because it might be on a test.

"Sometimes you even have to kill for peace," he says. "That's what history teaches us over and over. That's why I love history. That's why I teach it."

"He teaches history because he's too dumb to teach algebra," Ben Cooper says in a loud whisper. He sits right behind me in class, and he's talking into my ear. "He kept looking at all those equations with *x*'s in them. He wanted to know why they were using his signature over and over in a math problem."

I wish Ben wouldn't do this. He always tries to make me laugh in class. I laugh too easily and I cry too easily, and I don't think that's good. I need to get more control of my emotions. Like love, for example. I'm almost sure I'm in love with Ben, because I think about him all the time, and every time I see him I get sick to my stomach. If love makes you sick like that, I don't think it's good for you.

When Ben whispers something to me in class, I always stare straight ahead at Coach Morrison's bald head. I try not to smile or laugh. Coach Morrison hates it when students smile or laugh, unless he's telling a joke. He usually stops the class and asks what you're grinning about. I'd die if he did that to me. I might have to move to another state.

"Looks like Coach polished his big, bald dome this morning," Ben says. "If you look real close, you can see right through it."

"Stop it." I jam my elbow back and nudge Ben.

Fortunately Coach Morrison doesn't notice. He has a faraway look in his eyes. He's telling us how tragic it was that the Romans didn't have the guts to fight back.

"That's why they lost their empire," he says.

When the last bell rings, the halls are like a traffic jam. Everyone's laughing and screeching all around me. Ashley Skiles is grinning up at her boyfriend, Sam Boyd, while they walk down the hall. The way they're looking at each other, you'd think they were the only two people on earth. If they're not careful, they might run into a wall and get a brain concussion.

I'm walking right behind them, so I'm probably the only one who sees Ashley's right hand touch the left side of Sam's rear end and squeeze it. The two of them stop all of a sudden, and I bump into them. But they don't even notice me. They're kissing each other right in the middle of the school, with people walking all around them. If Ms. Heath, the school principal, catches them, they could get expelled. I might be forced to testify.

"Look at the hot couple!" one of the guys yells. Ashley and Sam pull apart, and they both smile, like they've got a big secret that nobody else knows.

I wonder what it feels like to put your hand on a boy's rear end. Sam's on the track team, so he has lots of muscles up and down his legs. His butt must be very muscular, too, kind of like thick pieces of rope. I know it's very disgusting to think about that, but I can't help it. Even though I've never had sex and at the rate I'm going I'll probably be a virgin when I die, I think I may be a sex addict. I think about sex all the time, especially when I'm trying to do my homework. If you're a girl and you're a sex addict, you're called a nymphomaniac. I looked that up in the dictionary two weeks ago, so I know what I'm talking about. I asked Mom what a male nymphomaniac was called and she said a fraternity brother.

I think being a nymphomaniac sounds very interesting. I could go around introducing myself like that. *Hi, my name's Sarah and I'm a nymphomaniac.* That way, people might pay more attention to me. I get tired of being ignored all the time.

I push open the door and walk outside. It's about

three hundred degrees. The sun's so bright, I have to squint so I won't go blind. Ellie's waiting for me by the steps.

Sometimes people say Ellie and I look alike. We're both tall and thin and we wear braces and have pretty bad posture. But Ellie's hair is light brown and long and straight, and mine is medium brown and shorter, and her eyes are brown and mine are green. Also, I have two medium-sized pimples on my face and Ellie doesn't have any. The truth is, we don't look really alike. It's just that most people don't notice either of us, so they get us confused all the time.

Ellie and I see each other about a hundred times a day, so we usually don't have much to talk about. Today, for example, we don't even say hello. We just glance at each other and start walking. It's pretty automatic. We walk to her house almost every day after school, since it's only six blocks away.

"My homework's going to take me hours," Ellie says. She pulls her hair back off her face and lifts it up in the air for a minute. "I'll never get it finished. I'll be up past midnight." She says that almost every day.

"Guess what?" I say. "Ashley Skiles was squeezing Sam Boyd's butt in the middle of the hall. In *public.* I was walking right behind them when it happened. I think I'm the only one who saw it. Then they kissed each other. I think their mouths were open, too."

"Oh, God, Sarah." Ellie heaves a big sigh. "Stop it. You're making me ill. Do you have to talk about all the grotesque people at that high school? We just spent the whole day there."

"It's a human-interest story. That's what we're learning about in journalism. I might have to write an article about French kissing someday. Or maybe butt squeezing. Can you imagine what the research would be like?"

"Stop." Ellie's cheeks are bright red, so she must be getting angry. I decide not to tell her that I may be a nymphomaniac. I don't think she'd be able to handle it.

Don't you think it's okay to have fun sometimes and gossip? I do. Some days I have to say things like this, or I might burst like a water balloon. If I didn't, Ellie and I would spend all our time having long, serious talks about homework and family problems and college and death-row inmates. Ellie's a very serious person. She likes to talk about social issues like capital punishment and juvenile delinquency and feminism all the time. She doesn't think about boys and sex twenty-four hours a day like I do. I hope that doesn't mean I'm a bimbo.

We keep walking, but we don't say anything for a while. It's kind of boring, so I stare at all the houses we walk past, even though I've seen them a hundred times. This is an extremely strange neighborhood, if you want to know the truth. All the houses have big lawns with perfect grass and flowers that are so bright they look like crayon colors. You never see people in these yards, unless they're gardeners. Most of the houses look like three-story fortresses, especially the new ones.

This suburb is called Hillside Park. I don't know why they named it that. We're right in the middle of Dallas, and you have to drive for about a thousand hours before you see anything higher than an anthill—unless it's one of the skyscrapers downtown. Prairie Park would be a lot more accurate, but it wouldn't sound as good. Also, our high school teams would have to be the Prairie Dogs, and that's not nearly as glamorous as the Hillside Park Buccaneers. I've seen prairie dogs at the zoo, and they don't have much personality. All they do is dig in the dirt and eat. Mom says they remind her of some of the lawyers she knows.

Almost everyone in Hillside Park is white and Republican and rich. Ellie says we should be ashamed of ourselves for living here, even though it's our parents' fault and we can't help it. She and I are the only Democrats I know. Like I said, Ellie's very socially conscious, and sometimes I am, too. When we get older, we're going to join the American Civil Liberties Union and Amnesty International. Right now, since we're only fourteen, all we can do is recycle soft-drink cans and write letters. Every time we read about someone who's on death row, we write the governor of the state where the prison is and ask him to spare the prisoner's life because of humanitarian principles. I don't think we've saved anybody's life yet, but it's important to keep trying.

We've been walking for ten minutes now, and Ellie and I still haven't said anything to each other. I guess she's waiting for me to say something. I glance at her out of the corner of my eye.

Ellie's staring down at the ground, the way she always does when she walks. She's frowning, but she doesn't look angry. That's good. She just looks sad and worried. That's the way she usually looks when we get closer to her home.

I think it's because her family is very messed up. Three years ago her father started acting strangely. He went to the gym every day and lost about thirty pounds. Then he bought a new wardrobe with lots of Italian suits and shoes and started getting his hair styled at a salon with a foreign name rather than going to an ordinary barbershop. After that he leased a new silver Porsche and went around telling people he wanted a simpler lifestyle. A few days later he moved out of the house and filed for divorce and started living with this woman named Misty, who used to be his secretary. Mom says that Mr. Peterson is the closest thing she's ever seen to a human cliché of a midlife crisis.

Last year Mr. Peterson and Misty got married, and they're going to have a baby in a few weeks. We're not supposed to say anything about them or the baby in front of Ellie's mother. I'm not sure why, since Mrs. Peterson talks about them all the time, anyway. She usually calls Misty "that dumb slut." Ellie says I should just nod when she says that so her mother can tell I know who she's talking about.

Mrs. Peterson and Ellie and Ellie's sister, Madeleine, live in a big house on Dartmouth. Mr. and Mrs. Peterson had the house built right before Mr. Peterson had his midlife crisis, so he only lived there for three weeks. It's made out of beige stucco and it has an orange tile roof, and it looks like most of the houses you see in Santa Fe. One time I heard Mrs. Peterson say that she'd burn the house down before she'd give it up. I'm just about positive that was a joke.

Ellie opens the front door and steps in. "Hello?" she says.

As usual, going into Ellie's house is like going to a

bowling alley. The stereo's on full blast upstairs and the phone's ringing and the dogs are barking outside the window. Something must be burning in the oven, because I can see a thin stream of black smoke coming from the kitchen. Ellie and I close the front door and follow the smoke down the entry hall.

No one's in the kitchen, but there are a bunch of burned cookies in the sink. They look like little pieces of charcoal, but they smell a lot worse. Ellie reaches for the phone, but it stops ringing. She sighs. She always sighs when she's upset.

Then she looks at all the smoke and burned cookies and shakes her head. "I guess Mom went on a bike ride," she says. "Do you want anything to eat?" I say no.

Ellie cleans off the kitchen counter with a sponge so we can sit down and study. That's what we do every day after school.

I can still hear the stereo playing really loudly, but Madeleine doesn't come downstairs. She's twelve and she's very moody. Sometimes she refuses to go to school and she stays up in her room for three or four days and plays lots of bad music on her boom box. Mrs. Peterson says the public schools don't appreciate Madeleine because she's so creative and artistic. That's why she keeps getting suspended all the time. Mrs. Peterson also says that if Mr. Peterson wasn't such a cheap, promiscuous, lowlife bagworm, he'd send Madeleine to a private school where her artistic persona would be appreciated. That's kind of a direct quote. I might use it for an article I'm writing in journalism about the state of family life in Hillside Park.

I put my hands over my ears so I can't hear Madeleine's music. I read my English assignment, which is to finish the last few chapters of *Jane Eyre.* I work on my algebra problems and do some exercises in my journalism book. I try not to think about Ben. I try not to think about sex, either.

By the time I finish my homework, it's almost six-thirty. Ellie and I haven't said much to each other the whole afternoon. I throw back my arms and stretch and yawn. I need to get more exercise. That's what Mom's always telling me.

"Gotta go," I say.

Ellie nods, but she doesn't look up. "See you tomorrow."

Outside, it's still light, but my shadow is long and thin in front of me. Maybe that means it's going to seem like fall one of these days. I hope so, since it's almost October.

Last week our newspaper had a big, bright picture of trees with orange and red and yellow leaves and a covered bridge with a dirt road winding up to it, and the cutline said, *Autumn! Glorious Autumn!* It was from New England, of course. When people want to illustrate the seasons, they never, ever come to Texas. The trees are pretty short here, and by the time they turn yellow, it's almost Christmas. Dad used to say that the only way you could tell it was autumn in Dallas was when all the women hauled their minks out of storage and wore them everywhere. When it's cold, you can see women walking around in full-length mink coats, doing their shopping at the grocery store. The animal-rights movement isn't very big around here. When we have more time, Ellie and I might start a local chapter. But so far, we've been too busy concentrating on the death penalty.

I love snow, but it only snows about once every million years in Dallas. We've never had a white Christmas here, either. Last year Dad and I were supposed to go skiing in Vermont after Christmas. I was excited, because I'd never been skiing before. But we didn't get to go. Dad had a heart attack after Thanksgiving and he died. The doctor said he died instantly. He said Dad didn't suffer at all. Doctors like to tell you things like that. Have you ever noticed? They like to tell you that someone didn't suffer, and you're supposed to believe them. But how do they know?

Sometimes people suffer and you can't even tell it by looking at them.

For a long time I used to dream about Dad every night. He and I would be standing together in this dream, and I would see him start to fall. I try to catch him, but I can't. I can't catch him or even touch him, and he keeps on falling. It isn't a very realistic dream, because I see him falling through the air, twisting over and over, but he never stops or hits the ground. He just keeps falling through the air, and no matter how hard I try, I can't help him. I keep trying to see his face and tell him I love him, but I can't do that, either. All I can do is watch him fall and get farther and farther away from me. After a while I can't even see him. It's like he's in outer space and he's so small and far away that I lose him in the stars.

For weeks after Dad died, I had that dream every night. I'd wake up, and I would be crying and my whole face would be wet. I cried when I was awake and I cried when I was asleep. I didn't stop crying for a long time after Dad died.

But that's changed. I've grown up a lot since then. I understand more than I used to.

When I think about Dad these days, I don't cry. I cry about other things, but I don't cry about Dad. I never dream about him, either. I just sleep hard. When I wake up in the mornings, I feel tired and sometimes I feel sad and I'm not sure why. If I've been dreaming about something, I never can remember what it is. Maybe I've forgotten my dreams. Or maybe I just don't have them any longer.

I think that's better, don't you? Dreaming can break your heart, if you let it.

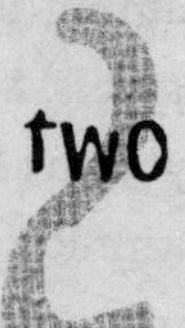

two

The house is empty when I get home. That's because Mom stays late on Thursdays so they can finish taping her TV show. The show's called *Dining with Dinah*, and it's been on TV for about a year. Mom's kind of famous in Dallas. Sometimes total strangers come up and ask her for her autograph. It's weird.

Inside, our house is completely different from the Petersons'. It's quiet and perfectly clean and it smells like furniture polish. If I ever have a drug overdose, it will be from inhaling furniture polish.

Mail's come through the slot and spilled on the Oriental rug in the entry hall, but none of it's for me. I almost never get letters, except from the governor of Texas. He's the only one who ever answers Ellie and me. He says he appreciates our concern for human rights, and he hopes we'll continue to be involved in politics when we grow up. I think he sounds nice. Ellie says to remember he's a Republican, though, and she's never known a Republican with a real heart, except for Abraham Lincoln, and look what they did to him. It was almost as bad as the Kennedy assassination, she says.

I'm making a peanut butter and mayonnaise sandwich in the kitchen when the phone rings. It's Nana, Mom's mother. She lives two miles away, and she always calls when she knows I'm here alone. I think it's because she likes to think that Mom's neglecting me.

"Are you all right, Sarah?"

I say I'm fine, and Nana goes on talking. She's seventy-five and she's mean, except you can't tell it till you get to know her. Dad always said she used to be a lot nicer before she started going to all those A.A. meetings. He said that if we were lucky, she'd start drinking again.

"I saw a program on latchkey children on TV last night," she's saying, "and I got so worried about you that I tossed and turned all night. One of the experts said that latchkey children have a 75 percent chance of going to prison someday. I think he was from Harvard. He had a very strange accent, but he seemed to know what he was talking about."

"I'm fine, Nana. I'm really fine."

"Prison!" Nana repeats. "I'm very concerned about you, Sarah. Do you want me to come over and stay with you? If your mother's coming home tonight, I could have a heart-to-heart talk with her about this man from Harvard. Maybe she'll listen to me for a change."

"I've got a lot of homework, Nana. I—"

"I'm very worried about you, Sarah. I think about you constantly."

Finally, after about three years, I get off the phone. Talking to Nana always makes me feel bad. I'm not sure why. I never say anything to Mom about how Nana calls me all the time. But I used to talk to Dad about it. One time he told me he had the perfect solution to long conversations with Nana.

"Next time she calls, you pretend you just speak Spanish, darlin'," he said. "The old bat hates foreigners so much, it'll probably give her a heart attack."

He and I started laughing when he told me that. I always laughed a lot when Dad was around. Everybody did. Dad told funny stories and said funny things all the time. He talked in a big, thick West Texas drawl and said *cain't* and *ain't*, and before he finished, people would be screaming with laughter and falling on the floor. Whenever Dad was around, there was always lots of noise.

Sometimes I think about all the stories Dad used to tell. I heard them over and over for years, and I know I remember them pretty well. I know they're the same stories that made everybody laugh when Dad told them. But when I think about the stories now, they're not as funny as they used to be. I don't know why. Even when I can almost hear Dad's voice telling them, they seem different. I hear the words slipping out—and I know they're the same words, the same stories I heard so many times—but they're not as funny any longer. I can hear the words, but I can't hear the laughter.

That's the difference, I guess. The stories are the same, but it's a lot quieter than it used to be when Dad was alive. Everybody's stopped laughing.

It's dark outside, and after I finish my sandwich I drag my backpack upstairs. It leaves tracks in the carpeting all the way up the stairs. Mom hates it when I do that. Our house is one of the oldest houses in the neighborhood, and the stairs have always squeaked. Sometimes, when I'm alone, that's the only sound I can hear. Mom says older houses that make noise have more character than new houses. She's very snobbish about things like character.

I turn on my desk lamp and computer. I still have one more assignment to finish for English. Ms. Evans wants us to write about how a modern-day Jane Eyre would act and think.

Ms. Evans is very young and kind of cute for a teacher, and she actually dresses all right. Last year she got married, but she kept her maiden name. That's what I'm going to do when I get married, because I'm a feminist, too. I'm pretty sure I can still be a feminist, even though I want a boyfriend. You wouldn't believe how women are discriminated against in our society, especially when they're in high school. You have to be thin and beautiful and popular, and that's all that counts. I'm tired of being discriminated against.

Anyway, Ms. Evans is a very good teacher and I like her, but I think this whole assignment is a bad idea. She says she wants to give our honors English class creative assignments like this so we'll be challenged. Every time I hear a teacher use the word *creative,* it makes me want to throw up. I don't think I'm creative. I have a very ordinary mind, and that's not good. I can tell Mom wants me to be more artistic, like her. Maybe if I start wearing black all the time, people will think I'm more artistic and creative. No, they'll probably just think I'm depressed. That's worse than being ordinary.

I'm still trying not to think about Ben. His arm brushed against mine after class, and it was very romantic. Maybe he'll call me sometime. Maybe he'll ask me for a date.

What if the phone rings right now and it's Ben? I'll have to pretend to check my schedule if he asks me for a date. That's what you're supposed to do when a boy calls. You're not supposed to act like you're hard up and completely desperate, the way I am. You're supposed to act like you have a very busy schedule and make little groaning noises about how full it is but ... *well, yes, you could ... possibly ... well, almost definitely ... go to a movie next week.* I practice making little groaning noises. They sound more like moans. I don't think I should moan like that when Ben calls. He might think I have a stomach virus or a toothache.

The computer screen goes blank and a bunch of white dots start floating around. It's very hard to concentrate these days. I may have attention deficit disorder. Maybe I should go on Ritalin like everybody else. It might make me calmer.

I grit my teeth and narrow my eyes so I can think better. This is a very strange assignment. A modern-day Jane Eyre. I try to think about Jane Eyre at Hillside Park High School. Which courses would she take? Where would she live? Would she still be an orphan? Would she be popular?

Headline: *Jane Eyre Elected Homecoming Queen.* Subhead: *Old-Fashioned English Girl Says She Never Heard of Football Till She Transferred to Hillside Park.*

No, that doesn't sound right. I don't think Jane would be the popular type. She's too nice. In fact, I don't think she'd fit in any better than I do at high school, especially around very mean, creepy people like Ashley Skiles and Emily Reif. It's also kind of hard to imagine Jane going to pep rallies or taking driver's ed, especially if she kept on wearing those long dresses. Someone would have to take her to Neiman's so she could open a charge account and start dressing better.

Wait a minute! I've got it! Maybe the twentieth century and Hillside Park High School would drive Jane completely nuts. She'd become so deranged that she'd join the Chihuahuas. That's it! That's much better! It's the most creative idea I've ever had in my life. I know how I'm going to start my paper, too: *Reader, I killed the cat.* Headline: *Hillside Park Student Confesses to Strangling Cat.* Subhead: *It Was Self-Defense, She Says.*

Jane Eyre, girl gang member. Jane Eyre, juvenile delinquent. For a good blow job, call Jane Eyre.

For a few minutes I feel happy. I love getting great ideas, even though I hardly ever do. Maybe I'm a little bit creative and interesting after all.

But then I realize that the paper might give me lots of problems. What if Ms. Evans calls the freshman counselor, Mr. Riggs, and tells him that I need to be put in a straitjacket? What if no one ever wants me to pet-sit again?

The front door slams and Mom yells hello. I look at my computer screen and it's still completely blank. I haven't written anything. I've always been very bad about daydreaming and now I'm getting a lot worse.

I've fallen in love and I'm taking antacids all the time and I'll probably get an ulcer and I'm practically flunking out of school. I'll have to go to work in a dime store or a car-parts factory. That's what happens to people who don't go to college.

Mom's saying something about dinner. I tell her I'll be a minute or two. I stare at my computer screen and then I write: *Jane Eyre: My Secret Life as a Chihuahua.* I center it on the page, then I put it in bold lettering so it's bigger. It looks very official. I save it on the computer, then I go downstairs.

Mom's cleaning the kitchen, even though it already looks fine. I always clean up after myself, because I know it drives her crazy if everything's not perfect.

Mom's tall and thin, and she has ash blond hair that she gets frosted every six weeks. She does everything fast. She walks fast and she talks fast and she cooks fast. I always feel slow when I'm around her. Mom's also very smart and witty. That's what everyone always says about her. *Your mother is so witty.* I never know what I should say when someone tells me that. I usually say thank you, though.

When I come in the kitchen, Mom looks up for a minute and kisses me on the cheek. "How was your day at school?" She rinses off her hands and dries them on a towel.

"Fine." Adults are always asking questions like that. I guess they feel like they have to say something. I haven't had a fine day at school in about a million years, but I always say everything's fine, anyway. Maybe someday it'll be true. Besides, it's better than complaining. I think complaining makes things worse. "How about yours?"

Mom shrugs. "About the same." She looks happy, though. She's dressed in a bright green suit with black trim and she has on lots of makeup, since she's just been filming her TV show.

I stay in the kitchen and talk to her while she makes dinner. Mom always seems happier when she talks to someone while she's doing a lot of work. That's why she's so good on TV, I think. She boils a big pot of water and drops some fresh pasta in. Then she brings some sauce out of the freezer and defrosts it.

I try to think of something to say. I tell Mom that I went over to Ellie's house after school, as usual. I tell her about reading *Jane Eyre* and writing an article about pep rallies for the school newspaper. I try to make my conversation interesting and funny and smart, the way Mom's always is. But I can tell it's not coming out that way. Everything I say sounds boring.

While I talk, Mom nods and says things like, "Oh, really?" and "Uh-huh." But I can tell she's not listening very closely. I wouldn't either, if I were her.

Every time I'm around Mom, I can tell she's disappointed with me. I'm quiet and I don't have lots of friends and, like I said, I'm a very ordinary person. Also, when I try to say something funny, it never comes out right. Especially when I'm talking to Mom. When we're together, I can always see that she's telling herself to slow down and be more patient with me. I think she tries to love me, but she wishes I was different. Most of the time I wish I was different, too. But I don't know what I can do about it.

Mom puts the pasta on some clay-colored plates she brought back from Mexico last year and pours sauce on the top. "Let's eat," she says.

She and I sit in the dining room. We twirl the pasta on our forks, and Mom finishes in about two minutes. She eats fast, too. I don't. I'm a very slow eater. It's probably some kind of symbol of my personality. People always say it's good to eat slowly, but then if you do, they sit around drumming their fingers and looking at you like you're personally ruining their lives. I don't think it's very healthy to eat while people are watching you. That's why I always tell Mom I'm finished before I am. I don't want to keep her at the table. She practically has a nervous breakdown if she has to sit still for five minutes.

We clean the kitchen together, and I tell Mom that I have to finish my homework. She kisses me good night, and for just a minute she looks at me in a funny way. Then she hugs me for a few seconds and touches my hair. Mom almost never does things like that. She hates people who go around touching and hugging and kissing all the time. Maybe she's had too much to drink.

For just a minute her face looks sad. She kisses me again on the forehead. "I love you so much, Sarah," she says. "Are you happy, baby? Are you okay?"

I guess Mom feels like she has to say things like that. She's been telling me she loves me a lot more often since Dad died. But I know she doesn't mean it. I can't explain how I know it, but I just do. I'm very sensitive about things like that.

"I'm fine." I pull away from her, but I try not to do it too quickly. "I've got to go finish my homework."

Mom's arms drop to her side. Her face looks sad again. "I know," she says. "I've got work to do myself."

When I get to the doorway, I turn and look back at Mom. She's already bent over a cookbook. Her head and shoulders make a long, dark shadow across the kitchen table. She doesn't seem to notice when I leave the room.

Mom and Dad got divorced three years ago, two years before Dad died. They weren't like Ellie's parents, though. They never said mean things about each other. I'm glad they didn't, but I wish they'd talked to me more about why they got divorced. Every time I asked Dad about why he and Mom got divorced, he looked sad.

"There's nothing you need to know about it, hon," he used to say. "It's between your mother and me. It just didn't work out."

I never asked Mom about it. She's not the kind of person who's easy for me to talk to, anyway. I was always much closer to Dad. But after a while I didn't ask him about the divorce, either. Even though Dad was one of the biggest talkers on earth, he wouldn't tell me why he and Mom got divorced. *It didn't work out.* That didn't tell me anything. I don't think it was fair, either, since I'm an only child. No one explained the divorce to me—not really—so I was the only one in the family who didn't know why it happened. It took me years to figure it out.

Ellie always thought my parents were still in love with each other, even if they didn't realize it. She says that you only fall in love—head over heels, passionately in love—once in your lifetime, and that divorce can be very romantic under the right circumstances. I don't know if that's true or not. But I knew Ellie was wrong when she used to say she thought my parents would get back together. I knew they wouldn't.

That's because I could see how much Mom was

changing. When she and Dad were married, she stayed at home and she was a lot quieter than she is now. After they got divorced, she went back to work. She started out as an assistant producer at the TV station and she worked all the time. She said she had to prove herself after staying at home for so many years.

It's funny when you see someone—especially your own mother—change so much. Some days I felt like she was a stranger, because she looked so different, so much stronger and happier. I'd never seen her that happy before. I guess I'd never realized that she hadn't been happy for a long time. I hadn't even thought about it. That was just the way she was—quiet and kind of sad. Sometimes she'd say very funny things, but she always talked in a low voice that no one listened to. Dad was the one who everybody noticed, and nobody ever paid much attention to Mom. Then they got divorced and everything changed.

When your parents get divorced, you're supposed to have this big fantasy about how they'll get back together and your life will be perfect. I never had that fantasy. That's because I knew Mom didn't need Dad any longer. Every time I looked at her, I could see that. We didn't have to talk about it, and she didn't have to tell me anything. I could see it and I knew what it meant. I think it's silly to have fantasies about something that's never going to happen.

Ever since my parents got divorced, I'm a lot more realistic than I used to be. It's better to be realistic, because that way, life doesn't surprise you so much. So I almost never have fantasies. But sometimes I have memories and I wish I didn't.

One of the memories I have is about what life was like when Mom and Dad were still together and we were all happy. They used to laugh and have a lot of fun. One time when I was about eight or nine, they got into a water fight with each other. Mom grabbed the backyard hose and aimed it right at Dad's face. He took the hose away and put it down the front of her shorts so the water spilled down her legs. I was in the kitchen, and I saw them in the backyard, standing in the grass, wet and laughing like two kids. I pulled a pot out of a kitchen drawer and filled it with water and went outside and threw it on both of them. Mom pushed Dad down, then he pulled us both down on top of him and rolled us over in the grass and tickled us. I can remember looking up at the sky and laughing while he tickled me as I tried to get away. The sun was going down and the sky turned pink and blue in streaks, and the three of us lay there on the grass and watched the stars come out and listened to the crickets chirp. Mom and I both lay with our heads on Dad's shoulders.

I don't know why I remember scenes like that, since

they're not really that important and they don't do me any good. I can remember laughing and rolling on the grass, and I know I was happy, but I can't remember what that felt like. That doesn't make very much sense to me. If I was remembering something that was very sad, then I know I'd feel sad remembering it. But I can't understand why I can remember something that was happy, when I felt wonderful, and that makes me even sadder. You'd think happy memories would make you feel good, wouldn't you?

I can still see us, wet and laughing on the grass on that summer night. I wonder if there was any one, certain moment when everything changed and we couldn't go back. I guess there was, but I just didn't notice.

three

"Will you listen to this?"

I'm listening. I'm in a stall in the girls' bathroom, and I have no idea who's talking. It's someone who's standing in front of one of the sinks. She's not talking to me, but I'm listening, anyway. I don't care.

I'm in a horrible mood today. I started out the day by dropping a cup of cappuccino in the cafeteria, and it splattered all over the place. It spilled all over the front of my beige blouse, which has to be dry-cleaned, and drenched two of my books. Practically every popular kid in my class was at the table next to me, and they all started laughing. I tried to smile and act like I thought it was funny, but I know my face turned bright red.

After that I cleaned off my blouse in the bathroom with a wet paper towel, but you can still see the stain. When I walked through the hall, I tried to hold my books really close so that nobody would see it. That's when I saw Ben standing at his locker, talking to another girl. I'm not even sure who it was. I turned my head to the side and started walking a lot faster. Ben didn't talk to me at all in world history. He's a very big creep. I don't know why I thought I was in love with him in the first place. If I ever saw his aptitude test scores, I would probably find out he's deeply retarded. Also, he might be a sexual pervert or a serial killer. Lots of high school boys are. I'm very lucky I've never been out on a date with him.

The minute the bell rang, I bolted out of world history. I went to English, and Ms. Evans was passing out our papers on Jane Eyre. I always get A's in English, but this time I got a C-plus. A C-plus! I'll probably have to run away from home with grades like that. *Interesting idea, but not very realistic*—that's what Ms. Evans wrote at the bottom of the last page. *Jane Eyre's a nineteenth-century feminist heroine and you've turned her into a modern cartoon figure. Do you really expect us to believe Jane would take a machine gun to a pep rally?*

After I read that, I realized I hate Ms. Evans almost as much as I hate Ben. I hate my whole life. I want to drop out of school, especially this mean, rich school. I think people put too much emphasis on education these days.

That's why I'm in the bathroom, eavesdropping. I may stay in this stall for the rest of my life. I'm a lot happier here than I am in the hallways.

"Are you listening?" It's the same voice again.

"Yeah," someone else says.

"Five guys–did you hear me?–*five guys* invited me to the homecoming dance."

Oh, gross. I know that voice. It's Emily Reif. I put my eye to the crack in the stall and peer out. Sure enough, I'm right. It's Emily talking to Ashley Skiles. Emily's brushing her hair and Ashley's putting on bright red lipstick. They both have so much blond hair that they look like a wheat farm. It's very bad for my self-esteem to see their hair. My hair's brown and it comes down to my chin and it's pretty limp. It might look better if I bleached it. One time, Mom's hairdresser told me I had a pretty face, but it was too bad about my hair. Mom said that Roberto was a good hairdresser, but no one had ever called him tactful.

"Five? Are you kidding? Who asked you now?"

The rest room door bangs shut. Emily and Ashley are gone. I don't even get to hear who asked Emily to the homecoming dance. Not that I'm really interested, but I'd kind of like to know. *Five boys. Five invitations.* I've never even gotten one invitation to a dance. I wonder what it would feel like to have your phone ring that many times and hear a boy's voice at the other end. It must feel great. One time a guy named Tom Stuart in my algebra class called to ask me what our assignment was, and I even liked that.

I come out of the stall and comb my hair in front of

the mirror. I wish I hadn't overheard Ashley and Emily. Emily's a very nasty person. When she sees you in the hall, she looks you up and down so you can tell she's checking out your clothes. Then she kind of sneers so you know that she thinks you have bad taste. Emily's mean to almost everybody, but she's very popular. It's strange. It seems like the worse she treats other people, the more popular she is. Every time there's an election, she wins it. I never vote for her, though.

Sometimes when I see girls like Emily and Ashley, I feel like they have so much power because they're beautiful. I wonder what it would be like to have that much power. You can almost feel it when they walk into a room, like they have a bright, hot light inside them that everybody can see and feel. We all notice them and stand up a little straighter and don't talk as much when they're around. Even the teachers notice, especially the men. Even somebody who's about five hundred years old, like Coach Morrison.

One time he called on Ashley in class and it was a very easy question, but she didn't know the answer. "I'm not sure, Coach," she said. Her voice sounded deeper than it used to, like she had a head cold. She looked up at him and tossed back her hair and smiled. I'm pretty sure she spent years learning to toss her head and smile like that. Coach Morrison turned red and he dropped his chalk on the floor and spent about fifteen minutes trying to find it. When he finally started lecturing again, he'd forgotten which civilization he was talking about. He kept calling the Romans the Romanians.

"That girl will go far," Ben whispered.

He was kidding, but the minute he said it, I knew he was right. Girls like Ashley and Emily do go far, and they go to places I'll never get to, like homecoming dances and parties and rides in convertibles on perfect days. Sometimes when I compare myself and my life to girls like them, I can't believe we live on the same planet.

I run a comb through my hair, but it doesn't do much good. Ashley and Emily might be gone, but you can still smell their perfume all over the place.

"My life is a disaster," Ellie says. "Mom's smoking again." School just let out, and we're walking to her house. "You know those long rides she takes on her bike? Well, I saw her yesterday and she was riding her bike and smoking a cigarette. She looked just like an ad for Virginia Slims. It was awful."

I never know what to say when Ellie gets upset about her mother. "At least she's getting lots of exercise," I say. "That's pretty healthy."

Ellie doesn't answer.

"So what're you going to do?" I ask.

"I don't know. Confront her, I guess."

Ellie is always talking about confronting her mother about something. Sometimes I think it's on her schedule. *Do homework. Feed dogs. Eat dinner. Confront Mom.* The trouble is, it never works. When Ellie tries to talk to her mother, she's very nice about it. But Mrs. Peterson usually ends up crying and saying she hates herself and she wishes she was dead. Then sometimes she goes to bed and won't get up. She stayed in bed for almost two weeks last spring. I think it was after she heard that Mr. Peterson and Misty were going to have a baby. Margaret, the Petersons' therapist, says Mrs. Peterson is going through a vulnerable period right now. She says Ellie and Madeleine need to be more supportive of her. Mrs. Peterson goes through lots of vulnerable periods.

Ellie and I walk along, and she tells me about a new study that shows the death penalty doesn't reduce the murder rate. It's the same study she told me about last week. "The death penalty doesn't help at all," she says. "It just brutalizes us as a society." That's also the same word she used last week—*brutalizes*. I think she must have read it in a magazine.

Ellie talks a lot more, but I don't listen too well. I'm thinking about Emily Reif. I wonder who she's going to the homecoming dance with. Maybe she should go with all five guys. That would show everyone how popular she is. She wouldn't have to hang around the girls' rest room brushing her hair and bragging about herself and giving other people indigestion.

When we finally get to Ellie's house, she's still talking about the death penalty and how terrible it is. The minute we open the front door, we can smell smoke, just like the last time. Mrs. Peterson is in the middle of the kitchen, smoking a cigarette.

"Mom, you promised—," Ellie begins.

Mrs. Peterson waves her arms around. She's very pretty for someone as old as she is. I think she's thirty or fifty. She has blond hair and blue eyes and one of those perfect noses with nostrils that flare. I wish I had a nose like that, instead of mine. My nose is way too big. It's about the size of a 747. I should have plastic surgery, but Mom doesn't believe in it. She says I'll get over worrying about my looks someday when I'm more mature. I don't think I'm ever going to be that mature.

Mrs. Peterson was voted one of the Ten Most Beautiful Girls on campus when she was at the University of Texas. There's a picture of her from that year that's right over the grand piano in the middle of the Petersons' living room. She looked exactly like a model.

Mrs. Peterson says that everyone always told her she looked like Cybill Shepherd or Candice Bergen, except a lot prettier.

"You can't expect me to ride around and smoke on my bicycle when it's this hot," Mrs. Peterson tells Ellie. "Besides, I'm under a tremendous amount of stress today, thanks to your father and his slut bride."

She inhales and blows out a big, white cloud of smoke. Then she waves her arms around again. She seems awfully nervous. I think she may have been drinking too much coffee.

Today Mrs. Peterson is wearing a burnt-orange caftan and she has blond bumps all over her head, where she's taken curlers out of her hair and hasn't combed it out yet. I've never seen her without makeup before, and she looks different. Her face is so pale that it's almost like it's disappeared. Her eyes look like the tiny dots you see on dominoes.

"I gave that bastard the best years of my life. The very best years of my life. Now I'm just old and wrinkled and tired, and he's having a baby with that two-bit tramp—"

The phone rings.

"I'm not talking," Mrs. Peterson says. She blows her nose loudly. "If that's your father, tell him I refuse to speak to him."

Ellie answers the phone and listens for a few

seconds. "She doesn't want to talk to you, Dad," she says. Her voice is soft and it sounds like there's something wrong with it. "No, I don't think right now is a good time."

Mrs. Peterson walks over to the phone. "You tell him," she says to Ellie, "that I refuse to buy a minivan. I have too much self-respect to drive a minivan. I'm not going to compromise myself. My therapist agrees with me on this."

"I guess you heard that," Ellie says into the phone. She listens more. "Uh-huh. Yeah, Madeleine and I are fine. That's right. Sure. We'll see you next weekend."

Later, when Ellie and I are in her room, I ask her about what happened. "Was that whole scene really about your mother driving a minivan?"

Ellie's eyes look funny, like she's older than Nana. She stares at me in a strange way. I feel like I just gave the wrong answer in algebra.

"Of course not," she says. "It's never about what they say it is."

The rest of the night we stay in Ellie's room and write letters. She's saved all the week's newspaper articles about convicts on death row. There's one in Georgia, two in Florida, and one in Texas. One of the men in Florida is called the Parakeet Murderer. He strangled a woman in her apartment, then he strangled her parakeet, too. *According to the police, the convicted murderer was afraid the parakeet could speak and identify him,* the article said. *Cruelty to animals is a misdemeanor in Florida.*

"We'll have to change our letter for that one," Ellie says. She's sitting in front of her computer screen and her face looks white from the glow. *Even though two lives have been taken, justice will not be served by taking a third,* she writes. *The victims of this horrible crime cannot speak for themselves, but we're sure they would want you to spare the life of this unfortunate man.*

I flop back on one of Ellie's twin beds. I feel tired all of a sudden. I feel sad, too. I don't know why.

Ellie and I have been best friends for three years, and I'm pretty sure we used to have more fun when we got together. But maybe that's wrong. Maybe we've always been friends because neither of us has anything better to do. Ellie usually says neither of us has had a date because there aren't any great guys at our school and our standards are too high. But that's not true. A few weeks ago, I made a list of all the guys I'd go out with if they asked me and it was almost two pages long, double-spaced. I don't want to tell Ellie, but I don't think my standards are high at all.

"You want to sign this?" Ellie asks. She hands me two letters to the governor of Florida. She's sitting in a purple chair, and she pulls her knees up in front of her and puts her head on top of them. Her hair's light brown and very straight, and Mrs. Peterson is always bugging her to get it highlighted.

I sign the letters and try to hand them back, but Ellie still has her face buried. So I put them on the computer desk. She doesn't say anything, and neither do I. I'm not sure why it's so quiet in the room.

I know I've probably hurt Ellie's feelings, because I'm not excited about writing these letters the way I used to be. I hate it when I do things like that. I always try not to hurt people's feelings, but sometimes I do, anyway.

I pull off my clothes and put on the T-shirt I sleep in. Then I get under the covers. Mrs. Peterson always keeps the temperature freezing cold in their house because she read that cold air prevents wrinkles. I hear the air-conditioning come on like a blast of winter air, then I turn over and fall asleep.

Ellie's bed is empty when I wake up in the morning. I get dressed and go downstairs. Madeleine's in the kitchen by herself, sitting on a barstool. She's Ellie's twelve-year-old sister.

"Where's Ellie?" I ask.

Madeleine shrugs and continues to eat her cereal. According to Margaret, Madeleine is in a nonverbal stage these days.

I kind of like Madeleine, but she's very weird, if you

want my honest opinion. I've thought that for a long time. For years all the drawings she put on the refrigerator showed people stabbing each other with long knives and swords and lots of bright red blood and gouged-out eyes. There's always a body in every picture. Madeleine loves to draw corpses, and she's very good at it.

Last spring Margaret asked her who the corpse in the picture was and Madeleine said it was her father. After that, all the corpses in Madeleine's drawings have been marked "Daddy," with an arrow pointing at them. Margaret told Ellie it was the biggest emotional breakthrough she ever had the privilege to witness as a therapist. Mrs. Peterson is very happy about it, too. She says it's restored her faith in therapy. For a while she was actually talking about having one of Madeleine's drawings framed so she could give it to Mr. Peterson and Misty for Christmas. I think Ellie talked her out of it, though.

Until this year Madeleine used to have normal-looking dark brown hair. But she dyed it red when school started, and now it's mostly red with long, dark roots and it points in lots of different directions. She wears black clothes and lots of black makeup on her eyes and she stares at the floor a lot.

Madeleine shoves a spoon in her mouth with her left hand. For a minute her sleeve slips back and I can see part of her arm. It looks horrible. It has lots of bruises and cuts on it, and it's red and swollen. Everything shows up really well because Madeleine's skin is so white.

"Jesus, Madeleine! What happened to your arm?"

Madeleine jerks her sleeve back over her arm. She looks up and glares at me, like I'm invading her privacy or something. "I ran into a rosebush," she says. She says that in a very calm voice, like she's talking about the weather.

For a minute we just stare at each other. I know Madeleine's lying, but I don't know what to say. What should I do—call the police or something? Write a letter to Ann Landers? Tell Ellie?

I feel so nervous and this is all so crazy that I burst out laughing. I always laugh when I'm nervous. It's a very bad habit.

Madeleine looks surprised. Then she starts to laugh, too. Her face crinkles up and she looks happy, for a change. She has beautiful eyes that look like blue crystal. It always surprises me when I see them. They don't seem to match the rest of her.

"What are you girls laughing at? What's so funny?"

It's Mrs. Peterson. She and Ellie are standing in the doorway. Mrs. Peterson still has her bathrobe on, and her eyes are red and her hair's messy. Her voice sounds high pitched, like it's about to break.

Mom's supposed to pick Ellie and me up in a few minutes, and I hope she's not late. I get very nervous when I'm at Ellie's house and Mrs. Peterson goes into one of her moods and screams and cries a lot.

"What's so funny?" Mrs. Peterson asks again.

Madeleine doesn't say anything. She gets up from the barstool and walks out of the kitchen.

"I'm speaking to you, young lady!" Mrs. Peterson screams. You can hear Madeleine run up the stairs and then her door slams. Mrs. Peterson sits on one of the barstools and starts to cry.

Ellie walks up to her mother and hugs her. Mrs. Peterson wraps her arms around Ellie's neck and the two of them are completely still. I can't even tell if they're breathing or not. I don't know what to do. I feel like I shouldn't be here. I hope no one notices me.

Somewhere in the distance I can hear a horn honking. It must be Mom. The horn stops, then it starts again. Mom's not the most patient person in the world.

"Ellie," I whisper. "Mom's here. We've got to go."

Ellie looks up at me and shakes her head. "I can't go." She looks like she's about to burst into tears, just like her mother.

I stand there for a few seconds. Then I pick up my overnight bag and purse and wave good-bye to Ellie. I don't know if I should say anything to Mrs. Peterson.

So I don't say a word. I just let myself out the front door and feel guilty because I'm so happy to get away.

Mom and I drive off, and I don't talk to Ellie for the rest of the weekend. When Mrs. Peterson gets like this, Ellie has to spend a lot of time taking care of her. She wouldn't have time to talk to me even if I called her. That's what I tell myself over and over. I'd like to talk to Ellie, but she doesn't have the time right now.

four

Today's Halloween, and Alex Baxter is giving a costume party at the country club.

Alex plays halfback on the junior-varsity football team. He's big and loud, and he has a round face. His father is the president of one of the biggest banks in town. I've known Alex since we were in kindergarten, and he's one of the scariest people I know. I know that sounds dumb, but it's true. I think he was born mean.

I don't know one person who's invited to Alex's party, but everyone in the freshman class knows about it. I'm not sure how we know about it, but we do. We know lots of details, like how Alex is dressing up like a heroin addict, with bloodshot eyes and fake needle marks in his arms and ragged blue jeans. That's Alex's idea of a very funny joke. I heard him say it was hard to decide between going to the party as a homosexual interior decorator or as a heroin addict, but he finally decided that heroin addicts had more fun, and he wouldn't want to act like he was gay, even if it was Halloween.

Alex and most of the other guys on the football team are very prejudiced against gay people, and they're always making jokes about pansies and limp wrists and hairdressers and AIDS. The way they talk is very disgusting. If Ellie and I had more time, we'd write the governors of every state about how homosexuals are discriminated against. We decided to try to save people on death row first, though, since Ellie said that was more of an emergency. But right now we're thinking about adding on a P.S. about gay rights and how homosexuals should be allowed to get married like everyone else, even if the governors don't want to go to their weddings.

Ellie and I both think it's important to make contact with people who are discriminated against. Ellie says it might make up for going to school with rich white kids all the time.

One time I told Roberto, Mom's hairdresser, that I fully supported gay rights. I'm pretty sure Roberto's gay, even though he's never said he is. He's fifty-three and he lives with a chef named Antoine, and one time I saw them walking down the street with their arms around each other. I hate to jump to conclusions, though. Maybe they're just good friends. But I wanted to let him know I wasn't bigoted, in case he was gay. I tried to make it sound very casual, like I was talking about the weather or something and not about him.

But I think Roberto caught on right away. He rolled his eyes and said, "Sweetheart, I've been liberated my whole damn life. I don't need the United States Supreme Court to tell me I'm all right."

"That shows how insecure he is," Ellie said. "Look—he couldn't even admit to being gay. You should bring it up again the next time he cuts your hair."

That was when Ellie was having lots of talks with Carmelita, the Petersons' housekeeper, about being a member of an oppressed minority. "She was so defensive, you wouldn't believe it," Ellie said. "She said she didn't have any problems being oppressed—but she thought *our* family was crazy. She said that every time she went to church, she said a special prayer for all of us. She said she's probably used up a gallon jug of holy water on our family, because we really need it. Do you think she was joking?"

"Probably," I said. *Probably not,* I thought. But I couldn't tell Ellie that, of course. She always gets upset if anyone criticizes her family. That's why I haven't said anything to her about all those cuts and bruises I saw on Madeleine's arm. She might tell me to mind my own business or something.

I'm not going to Ellie's house after school today. She and Madeleine and Mrs. Peterson go to see Margaret every Tuesday and Thursday, so we never walk home together on those days. I wave at Ellie when I see her in the hall, but we don't talk.

I also see Ben in the hall three times. I decide that I'm still in love with him, because I feel dizzy every time I see him. He must have gotten his hair cut yesterday, because it's shorter. It springs up on his head, but it looks soft. I wish I could reach out and touch it without anybody noticing, just to see what it feels like. Maybe I could pretend like I was just bumping into him. Even though it makes me a little nauseated, I always feel better when I'm thinking about Ben. Most days it's the only thing I feel like doing.

That's because I have about a million problems right now. I'm not sleeping much and I cry a lot and practically the only person who calls me on the phone is Nana. Also, I'm under way too much stress at school.

In journalism I asked Mr. Daniels if I could do an investigative piece on graffiti and smoking in the girls' bathroom. I told him I'd have to have a pass so I could spend the whole day in a bathroom stall for my research. I thought that sounded like an extremely good idea, because I'm tired of going to all my classes. Mr. Daniels said that I needed to think a lot more about my article. Then, when I had a more realistic idea, I could come back and talk to him.

That's another thing that's wrong with this school.

No one likes students who have unusual ideas. This whole place likes to think it's very creative, but it's not. It's very repressive. I might as well be going to school in Russia.

Then, in English, I had to write two papers about mythology. Ms. Evans made us create original gods or goddesses, then we had to describe them and write about their lives. I wrote about Emilia, the goddess of bleached blondes. *Her heart was even darker than her roots,* I wrote. I thought that was a very good line. Maybe I'll be a writer when I grow up. *Emilia was a very evil, vicious goddess who had the morals of a French poodle. She lived in a room filled with mirrors so she could watch herself twenty-four hours a day. Emilia thought that was even better than watching television, which she also did a lot of, because she was very superficial and she had a pathetically low IQ.*

I was feeling extremely creative when I wrote that paper, but I had to turn it in before it was completely ready. So I didn't write much more. Ms. Evans gave me a B-minus. *Sarah,* she wrote, *next time why don't you try whimsy instead of character assassination?* I don't think Ms. Evans likes me much. At the rate I'm going my grade point average will be terrible.

Fortunately when I get to English today, I find out that Ms. Evans is sick. We have a substitute who's tall and thin, like a stork, and she has black hair pulled back into a bun.

"I'm Miss Lester," she says. She writes her name on the board and the chalk squeaks. Then she turns around and faces us. She's biting her lower lip, and she seems nervous. I don't think she's had much experience teaching. "We're going to be continuing with Ms. Evans's lesson plans. You're discussing mythology, aren't you?"

Robert Adams raises his hand. He's a good friend of Alex's, but he's much smarter. He's also the best-looking guy in the whole freshman class. He has dark hair and brown eyes, and every time I look at him I feel like I need to take a deep breath. I wish I didn't notice how good looking he is, but I do. Sometimes I look at Robert and wonder about him. You'd think that someone as nice looking as he is would be a nice person, wouldn't you?

"Pardon me, Miss Lester," Robert says. Even his voice is handsome. It's low and smooth, like a TV announcer who wants to sell you panty hose that don't run. "Didn't Ms. Evans tell you she changed our lesson plans? She decided she was sick of teaching mythology after all these years. She said she wanted us to read something more modern. Something more relevant to our lives—that's what she said."

Miss Lester frowns and looks at her notes. "Well, I—"

"She didn't tell you?" Robert asks.

Miss Lester shakes her head slowly. She looks like

she's drowning, but she's too polite to mention it. You can also tell she's noticed how good looking Robert is.

Robert frowns and looks concerned. "She was very clear about it last week. She said she hated the Greek and Roman gods. She felt we were wasting our time reading about them."

"Yeah," Alex says loudly. "She wants us to read anything we want. I'm gonna read *Candy*. Ms. Evans thinks pornography is really good for you." He pronounces *pornography* wrong, with the accent on the first syllable. Robert looks like he wants to kill Alex for being so dumb and spoiling the joke.

Lots of people in the class start to laugh, and Miss Lester's cheeks turn bright red. She stares down at her notes for a long time and doesn't say anything. I think she's trying to take deep breaths and calm down. That's what Mom does sometimes before she goes on TV.

Finally Miss Lester looks up at us, and her face is still red and her hands are shaking. I can see them shake and hear the paper rattle and, for a minute, I feel so terrible that I can't stand it. I've been laughing with Alex and Robert and everyone else in this stupid class. I used to be a good person, and I don't know what's happened to me. Today I'm acting as mean as everyone else.

"Would anyone like to tell me," Miss Lester asks,

"about the Greeks' sense of morality?" Her voice is shaking, just like her hands.

After dinner Mom and I go to the grocery store to get candy for the trick-or-treaters. By the time we get back from the store, it's dark and you can see kids and their parents on the sidewalks and streets. Some of the mothers around here spend weeks making their children's Halloween costumes so they can win prizes at school. Mom says it's all Martha Stewart's fault. She thinks Martha Stewart has probably set feminism back a couple of centuries and that graduate students will write dissertations on her evil influence for years.

We empty the candy into big salad bowls. "Did we remember to get some carrots and celery for all the little anorexics in the neighborhood?" Mom asks. She starts to laugh and so do I, even though I don't think you should laugh about people with diseases.

Nana is always saying that Mom makes fun of everything, and someday she's going to fry in hell for it because God doesn't like jokes. "All you have to do is read the Old Testament to find that out," she told me last year. "You remember the story about Abraham and Isaac? God wasn't kidding around when he did that, Sarah. God doesn't kid around."

My parents never went to church and I never read the Bible, so I didn't have any idea who Abraham and

Isaac were. So later I asked Dad what Nana was talking about. Dad's parents were Southern Baptists and he knew everything about the Bible.

Dad said that God was trying to see if Abraham really loved him. So he asked him to kill Isaac, his only son. "One of them dumb-ass passages I never did get," Dad said. I remember how he snorted and exhaled a bunch of cigar smoke.

"What's the old bat doing, telling you about Abraham and Isaac?" Dad snorted again. He always snorted a lot when he talked about Nana. "She ain't busy enough these days, goin' to her Daughters of Hitler meetings? Christ almighty, I wish that woman would start drinking again." Dad said that in his opinion, Nana was wrong about God not having a sense of humor. If he didn't have one, he wouldn't have invented the institution of marriage.

That was almost a year ago, right before Dad had his first wreck. A year ago. That's hard to believe, because it seems so much longer. Dad ran into a telephone pole and smashed up his car, but he walked away from the wreck and he was just fine. He made a joke out of the whole thing. If you'd heard him tell it, you would have thought it was funny. Most people did.

I stand there, picking up the pieces of candy again and again and letting them slide through my fingers, while I think about Dad. He was still alive a year ago. Only a year. I can't believe it's not longer than that. It feels like a million years.

Sometimes I think I was a different person then. Everything was so clear and simple to me. Then Dad died and everything changed—and nothing seems clear or simple any longer. That's what happens when you grow up, isn't it? You see things differently. But I didn't want to grow up! I didn't want any of this to happen! I wanted everything to stay the same, because it was good, it was wonderful, the way it was. I miss everything I used to have. I miss being happy and laughing all the time. Why did everything have to get so damned complicated and hurt so much? Why did Dad—

All of a sudden the doorbell begins to ring and then it rings again. It doesn't stop for an hour. I go to the door and hand out candy to ghosts and fairy princesses and elves and pirates who stand in the porch light and hold out their bags. Mom stays in the dining room, going over a script.

The later it is, the older the trick-or-treaters get. Most of them are from the south part of Dallas, and they're black or Hispanic. They like to come to this neighborhood because it's safe and people give you lots of candy. Lots of our neighbors don't like these kids. They say they should stay in their own neighborhoods. That's why they turn off their lights and pretend not to be home. So I always try to give lots of candy to those kids. They usually just wear a mask or maybe a sheet, and they almost never say thank you. But they seem to be so excited about Halloween. They laugh and talk and hold out their bags, and then they run off into the darkness.

Every year I see kids like this, and I try to give them more and more candy. I hope that helps, but I don't think it does. I want to make up for their lives and how poor they are, but I don't know what to do. I stand there in that door, with the porch light on, and I know how I must look to them. I look rich and warm and well fed, and I'm dressed nicely and my house is big. I want to make some kind of contact with these kids and let them know that I have all of that and I know they don't, and I know my life looks perfect and easy, but it's not. Sometimes I feel like my heart is breaking. Maybe it's not really breaking for other people, though. Maybe it's just breaking for myself.

Standing there, in the porch light, I look out into the darkness. I feel so sad, I want to die. I know why. It was a year ago, exactly, when my life started to tear apart.

How do I make sense of all this? I can't. That's why I

don't want to think about it. Because it doesn't make sense. I still need Dad and I'll always miss him. But he's gone. He's gone forever. He shouldn't have left me when I needed him so much. It wasn't right. For just a minute I let that in, like a brief bit of light, but it hurts my eyes and slams into my heart, and I have to let it go.

I turn off the porch light and lock the door and then I sink down on the floor. I lay my head on the floor and put my hands on my head and try to breathe calmly. If I have to, I'll stay here all night. It's better than going to bed and lying there for hours with my eyes open, alone in the dark.

Sometimes I feel like I'm reliving my life this time last year. I go over everything that happened to me so I'll understand it better. All of this is hard to explain. But I'll tell you what I know is true.

I loved my father more than anyone else I've ever known. When I was little, I thought he was the biggest man in the world. Even when I got older, I still thought the same thing. Dad was bigger than anyone else I knew. When he died, the coroner's report said he was only five-eleven, but I don't think that's right. Maybe it's hard to measure people after they're dead.

I don't want to talk about Dad when he was dead,

though. I want to make you understand what he was like when he was alive and why I loved him so much. He filled rooms. I know that sounds strange, but I mean it. When he came into a room, it changed because he was there. Other people changed when they were around him, too. Everyone started talking more and laughing more and having a better time when Dad was there. Even Mom knew that. "There's some kind of magic about your father," she said one time. I can still see the way she looked when she said that. Her lips were stretched into kind of a funny smile, but her eyes looked sad.

Magic. That's the perfect word. Dad had magic. But I can't explain his magic. The truth is, I don't think you should even try to explain something like that.

One time when I was about six, I saw a magician when I was with Nana. For his last trick the magician pulled a rabbit out of his hat. Nana started complaining about how that was the oldest trick in the book and every magician did that same dumb trick. She kept talking about that while we left the theater, but I didn't listen to her. I was thinking about the rabbit in the hat, and how silky and alive it was. I didn't want to listen to what Nana was saying and I never wanted to try to figure out how the magician got the rabbit into his hat. I didn't want to know. I don't think you can focus on two things—the trick and the magic—at the same time. I didn't care about the trick then, and I still don't. I don't think magic should be explained. It just *is.* Maybe you should just believe in something because it makes you feel happy and alive. Maybe you don't have to understand it. Maybe it hurts when you understand too well.

So, all I can do is tell you about Dad's magic, because that was all I ever saw. Even when I think back, it's the only thing I want to see.

He was the biggest person in the world then.

He was magic.

I know I said I want to tell you what's true, and this doesn't sound true at all. But to me it is. The truth is, I believe it with all my heart.

I think it was this time last year that Dad and I went out to dinner for one of the last times. We went to a restaurant called Star Mesa. It has copper walls and cactus hanging down from the ceiling and tables that look like they're made out of rocks. The menu has lots of local dishes like chicken-fried steak and enchiladas and venison barbecue. Mom had just been there two months before, and she said the food wasn't that great—just overpriced. "Ever since Mick Jagger vomited in the women's bathroom, it's been crowded," she said. "I'd like to know where Mick Jagger *hasn't* vomited." Mom's very picky about restaurants.

Dad ordered a bourbon on the rocks and I asked for a Coke with lime in it. When our drinks came, we touched our glasses together and toasted. We always did that when we were together, ever since I can remember.

As usual, Dad asked me about school. Was I doing all right? Was I happy? Were my teachers good? Lots of grown-ups ask you questions like that, but Dad was different. He actually wanted to know the answers. He sipped his drink and watched me. He had big, bushy eyebrows and green eyes that looked like marbles.

I told him that school was all right and my classes were fine. I stirred my drink with the red swizzle stick and watched the lime bob up and down. "I feel so lonely sometimes. I feel like such a loser. Everybody's prettier than I am or smarter. I've still never had a date."

Dad shrugged. "You've got your whole life to date, darlin'." He pointed to his glass and ordered another drink. Then he winked at me. He always winked at me, like we were the only two people on earth who knew a very funny joke. "Besides, any boy too dumb not to ask you out ain't worth pissin' on."

When Dad talked like that around Nana, she used to say he was crude. That always made Dad happy. He'd drink more and more and talk worse and worse.

Dad said he couldn't help it. The sight of Nana's ugly face just made him feel like drinking and cussing.

One time, when we were at Nana's for dinner about four years ago, Mom went home early and Dad drank a lot more than usual. He said it was because Nana was getting on his nerves. After a while he passed out on Nana's best Oriental rug, with a bottle of bourbon hugged to his chest. I was in the living room, pretending to be asleep on the couch, and I heard Nana calling the police.

"I wish to report a crime," she said. "A drunken man is prostrate on the extremely valuable antique Tabriz in my dining room. I'm in fear for my life."

The police rang the doorbell a few minutes later, and Nana let them in. By then I was tired of pretending to be asleep and I watched everything over the top of the couch. It was a lot more interesting than any program you could see on TV that year. Nana led the policemen into the dining room and pointed at Dad. "Arrest this man for public inebriation," she said. She was using her Vassar accent. She always used that accent when she wanted to boss someone around.

Dad opened one eye and grinned at the two police officers. He knew them both, of course. Dad knew everyone. He sat up very slowly and shook their hands. "Been a long time since I've seen you boys," he said. "You doin' all right?"

They said they were, and Dad asked them about their wives and kids. Nana just stood there with her arms crossed, getting angrier and angrier. Finally she asked the police officers why they weren't arresting Dad for public intoxication. They just stared at her.

"He's not in public, ma'am," one of them said. He shifted back and forth on his feet. He and his partner both looked embarrassed. They didn't know what to do.

"Oh, shitfire," Dad said. He took a long drink out of the bourbon bottle and handed it to one of the policemen. "Hot damn. *Excusez-moi,* Pierre. I'm forgettin' my goddamn manners. I haven't introduced you boys to my mother-in-law." He pointed up at Nana. "This is Mrs. Jeffers, boys."

The two police officers took off their hats and said hello to Nana. You could tell they weren't used to having someone formally introduce them to the person who was trying to have him arrested. Then they continued to shift from one foot to the other. It was almost like a dance. They didn't laugh, but you could tell they wanted to. I could tell that Nana knew that, too. She's never been smart about other people, but she isn't stupid, either. Nana shook their hands very grandly. After a few seconds she turned around and marched up the stairs.

I don't think Dad knew I was watching all of this.

But maybe he did. He usually acted the same, no matter who was around him. I watched for a few more minutes, while both the policemen sat down on the Tabriz and started passing the bourbon bottle back and forth. Dad brought out big cigars for them to smoke and, after a while, they were all laughing and clapping each other on the back and drinking so much they could hardly sit up.

I fell asleep for about an hour, till I heard gunshots. I looked outside, and Dad and the two policemen were pointing their pistols at the streetlights, trying to shoot them out. I couldn't see their faces. I could just see their silhouettes shifting and swaying back and forth against the street. They were way too drunk to hit anything, but they kept on raising their pistols and firing again and again.

I heard Dad tell that story about how Nana tried to have him arrested about a hundred times. Everyone always laughed. I laughed at it, too. I guess you could say it's not very funny, and maybe it's not. I guess you can tell the same story in all kinds of ways, and make it happy or sad or angry or terrible.

But that's not why I'm telling this story. It doesn't matter if it's funny or not. I want to tell you what life was like when Dad was around so you can understand how I felt about him, and that's one of the best examples I can think of.

Things like that were always happening to Dad. The colors were brighter and the sounds were louder and everything seemed bigger and funnier and wilder. I can still see the three of them, swaying in the street. They were too drunk to hit the streetlights, but maybe they weren't even aiming at them. With Dad around, they might have been shooting at the sky.

five

"You think you have problems?" Coach Morrison asks the next morning. It's first period, and I'm trying to stay awake. I only got about two hours of sleep last night. That's why I'm propping my face on my hands and trying to look alert.

Coach Morrison glares at our world history class like we're a bunch of Communists who want to take over the Alamo. He's been in a horrible mood this whole week, ever since the football team lost 63–0. The newspaper said it was the worst defeat in Hillside Park history.

Most of us look down at our books so we won't have to look at Coach. When he's in a terrible mood like this, it's not good to look at him. He might call on you and ask some question that's impossible to answer so he can give you a zero for class participation. I leaf back and forth in my book. We're supposed to be talking about the Phoenicians today. At least I think we are.

"You kids don't have any problems," Coach Morrison says. "My generation had real problems. The Phoenicians had real problems. You don't know what real problems are—"

"The football team knows what real problems are," Ben whispers. "Duh. Sixty-three to nothing. That's higher than the whole team's IQ."

"—Depressions. Wars. Plagues. Assassinations. Polio shots. We had to be tough when I was growing up. The Phoenicians had to be tough, too—"

"It was really tough when the Phoenicians found out they weren't living in Phoenix, Arizona," Ben says. "I don't think Coach knows that yet."

I dig my fingernails into Ben's knee and he jerks his leg back. I try to ignore him, but I don't want to listen to Coach Morrison, either. I can tell he's getting all wound up, and he's getting angrier and angrier. That happens to teachers around here sometimes. They decide that everyone in the whole school is a bunch of snotty, spoiled rich kids who don't have problems. Sometimes our parents say that, too.

I don't think it's true, though. Well, not completely. There are lots of kids who are snotty and spoiled and rich at Hillside Park, but a lot of us have problems, too. I think I'll write an article about that for my journalism class. Maybe I can take a poll, too. *Forty-Five Percent of HPHS Students Are Deeply Depressed*—that would make a nice headline. Maybe I could interview myself for it if I change my name. I could call myself an unidentified source. Lots of journalists do that.

Nana's always telling me I should count my blessings, like having a nice house and a grandmother like her. She says the Lord helps those who don't lie around whining about their lives. Nana goes to the Second Baptist Church, and she's always trying to get me to go to church with her. She says I'd be a lot happier if I got to know the Lord. Every week she asks her Sunday school class to pray for me.

Nana told me I need to pray even more than I used to, since I'm so upset about Dad dying. She said if I gave my life over to the Lord, he'd help me understand that everything happens for a reason. That's what she says, "Everything has its own reason, Sarah. You just don't know what it is yet. But you will someday."

I know she means well and she's trying to love me, but she doesn't understand at all. She never understood what Dad meant to me, and I don't think I've explained it well enough to you, either. But let me try again.

In my life, everyone wants me to be something that I'm not. Nana wants me to be religious. Mom wants me to be smart and ambitious and funny. Ellie wants me to be more like her, really serious, with a big social conscience. My teachers want me to be creative and smart. I even want to be something I'm not, because I don't like the way I am.

But when Dad was alive, it was different. Every time I was with him, I felt so good and comfortable. I felt like I could be anything or anyone I wanted to be, and it would be fine with him. If I dyed my hair green or got a body tattoo that said *Buzzzzz!* or dropped out of school to become a tightrope walker, that would have been fine with him. He would have looked at me and grinned the way he always did and said, "Fine with me, darlin'. As long as you're happy." Then he would have winked, like we both understood something that no one else did.

I read an article one time that talked about *unconditional love.* It said that kind of love is when you don't have to do anything or be anything for another person. You're just loved, no matter what. I read that article three or four years ago, but I still remember it. When I saw it, I knew it was describing Dad and the way he loved me. *Unconditional love.* That's what it was, but I'd never known the words to describe it before.

That's what Dad was like for me. That's the best I can explain it. When he was alive, I knew he'd love me no matter what. It was a part of me, like breathing, and then I lost it.

But I remember it so well. I catch myself leaning

back and remembering things, like that night with him at Star Mesa, and how he pulled out a cigar after dinner and lit it with a match and sat back and smiled at me. The light was dim, but I could see the wrinkles in his face when he smiled at me.

I smiled back at him. I could see my reflection in the mirror across the room, and I knew that I wasn't beautiful like all the other girls I knew, and I knew I'd never be beautiful. But for a few minutes it didn't matter. I didn't have to do anything. All I had to do was sit there and smile back at my father, and everything was fine. I watched the pale white cloud of his cigar smoke float higher and higher, rising toward the ceiling.

I remember how Dad put his hand around my neck and kissed the top of my head then. "You make me happier than anything else in my life, darlin'," he said. "You remember that, hon. Nothing else comes close."

He hugged me again and I kissed him on the cheek, and I can remember exactly how I felt. When I was with Dad, I felt safe and loved and warm. No matter what happened, Dad would take care of it. As long as he was there, everything would be all right. Everything would be fine.

I thought Dad would always be with me and he would always make everything all right. I loved him more than anyone in the world, and I'm going to miss him every day for the rest of my life. No matter how old I get, I'll never get over losing him. I know I won't. People are always saying that time helps grief and then they start talking about emotions and scars and healing, and I want to scream when I hear them say things like that. Time hasn't made me feel any better. And I don't have scars and I never will. All I have are these memories that take me back to a time when I was happy and I knew someone else loved me more than anything in the world. I had all of that and now it's gone forever. Sometimes I can't stand to think of that time or of Dad, because it hurts too much. I can't stand to think about everything I used to have, and how it's gone and it's never coming back. I can't do it.

I shut my eyes and try to breathe regularly. That's supposed to calm you down and make you feel better. Today it doesn't work, though. I want to put my head on my desk and cry about everything that's gone. I could cry the whole day. I know I could. I have tears in my eyes and I keep blinking them. I can't let myself cry at school.

"Close your books," Coach says. He looks angry and tired and sad, all at the same time. I don't think he's sleeping any better than I am. "We're having a pop quiz."

* * *

That night Ellie calls after dinner.

"Misty just had her baby," she says. "He was two weeks early."

"That's great." I'm not sure if it's great or not, but you have to say things like that. People want you to act very happy when they have babies or get married, even though you might not think it's a good idea.

"Yeah. Dad called us about it. He sounded really excited. He said he's always wanted a son."

While Ellie talks about the baby, I sit and stare at my computer. The screen is blank, as usual. I still haven't come up with a title for my English paper. I can tell I'm going to be up very late tonight.

We're supposed to write a haiku about an American hero. I think I'm going to write about Mario Cuomo. You may not have heard of him, but he used to be the governor of New York and he's very liberal. He's against the death penalty, too, just like Ellie and me. He's also very sexy. But it's going to be very hard to work all of that into a haiku. I wonder if Ms. Evans will notice if I squeeze in a few more syllables. Sometimes you have to do things like that.

Most of the girls in the class are writing haikus about John F. Kennedy, even though they're Republicans. I don't think that's fair. If you're going to be a Republican, then you should have to write a haiku for some Republican politician. Then maybe you'd figure out that there aren't any Republicans you'd ever want to write a haiku about in a million years. Maybe you'd realize you should become a Democrat instead, because their politicians are a lot better looking and sensitive.

Even though I'm a Democrat, I wish Ms. Evans wouldn't give us so many creative assignments. I'm tired of being creative. I want to be boring. I wish she'd ask us to count the number of commas in a poem. I'd probably make a better grade that way.

Ellie's stopped talking. The line's silent and, for a few seconds, I panic. I don't know what she's been talking about and I don't know what to say to her. We used to talk on the phone for hours and hours, and it used to be fun. But now I can't think of anything to say to her.

"It should be fun having a little brother," I say. "I like babies. Maybe we can baby-sit him sometime."

"Yeah." She sighs. "Mom's pretty torn up about it. She's been crying for hours. She says she's pretty sure Dad divorced her because they didn't have a son. That's why she's so upset about this."

I wonder if that's true. I've heard about men who get depressed if they don't have a son. I think it's called testosterone poisoning or something like that, and it makes them feel a lot better to throw a football around or tackle other people or make a lot of grunting noises. Mr. Peterson used to be a quarterback in high school, so maybe he has testosterone poisoning.

"Could you ... maybe come over tomorrow after school?" Ellie asks.

I haven't been to Ellie's house in three days, and I don't want to go tomorrow, either. But I know I need to. I tell her yes, I'd love to come over tomorrow.

Sometimes when I'm with Ellie, it seems like we don't have very much in common. And maybe we don't. But I always try and remind myself why we've been best friends for so long. We started being best friends in the sixth grade. That's the year Ellie's parents got divorced and so did mine. I guess we were both lonely that year. We sat by each other in school, and we just seemed to get along right away. It was nice to have a friend who understood what my life was like even when I didn't want to talk about it.

Ellie's one of those people you appreciate more and more the longer you're around her. It took me months to understand the most important thing about her—that she always tried to protect other people. I didn't understand that for a long time, till I'd seen it over and over and I couldn't mistake it. I saw it in her face and in everything she said and did. She'd throw herself in front of a bus before she'd hurt another person.

That's something I never want to forget about Ellie. It's too important. She's a much better person than I am, and she's been a wonderful friend to me. I can't forget that.

When Dad died, she was the only person I could talk to. Every night, even after I'd been at her house in the afternoon, she called me and asked how I was. No one else did that. Not even Mom. Sometimes I'd see people staring at me in the halls, and they'd look away when I turned around. Most people didn't want to talk to me at all. Or if they did, they acted like nothing had happened. Or they were a lot nicer than they used to be. For a while, even Nana was nicer. But almost nobody said anything about Dad, except for Ellie. It was like he'd disappeared and no one but me noticed.

Sometimes when Ellie called, I couldn't even talk. I'd just cry. Ellie wouldn't say anything, but I knew she was there, listening to me. "Are you all right, Sarah?" she'd ask me. And after a while I'd say yes, I was all right.

When I get impatient with Ellie, I always make myself think about those times and what a good person she is. She was the only friend I had then, and she was the only one who was trying to understand me. She's the best friend I'll ever have.

Like I said, it hurts to think about that time and I

hate to do it. But sometimes you have to make yourself remember what's important. Do you know what I mean? It's hard, but you have to do it. You have to keep reminding yourself of what's important. You can't let yourself forget. If you don't remember what's important, then something bad might happen. You might make some kind of terrible mistake.

six

Friday night Ellie and Madeleine and I go to dinner at Mr. Peterson and Misty's house. They live in a new, two-story house that's redbrick and stone and has three trees that were just planted in the front yard. There's a brand-new welcome mat at the front door. The minute Mr. Peterson opens the door, I can smell potpourri. I'm glad Mom's not here. Whenever she's around potpourri, she makes lots of gagging noises and claims she can't breathe.

"Come in, girls!" Mr. Peterson says. He's balding and he has pale blue eyes, and he likes to stare right into your face when he shakes your hand. He also likes to squeeze your hand very hard, like he's testing how strong you are. "Meet the newest member of our family!"

Mr. Peterson's carrying the baby against his shoulder. It's the tiniest baby I've ever seen, with a little pink head and curled-up fists. He's dressed in light blue pajamas with a matching blanket wrapped around him. He's asleep, and you can hardly tell he's breathing.

"Edward Blake Peterson Jr.," Mr. Peterson says. He pulls the baby back onto his shoulder and smiles at us. "I've waited for this day for a long time."

Ellie reaches out a finger and touches the baby's small fist. "He's beautiful, Dad."

"Yeah," I echo. The truth is, I think the baby's very weird looking. His head is kind of pointed. It's almost shaped like a football.

Madeleine stares down at the floor. She has dark silver eye shadow smeared all over her lids, and last week she dyed her hair black. It looks like the dark part of a skunk's fur. She opens her mouth and yawns very loudly. "Can we watch TV?" she asks.

Mr. Peterson ignores her. He pulls the blanket over the baby's head and smiles at us. I don't think I've ever seen him this happy. It's very strange, like he's almost turned into a different person. "We're going to call him Blake," he says. "It's bedtime right now. Tell these girls good night, Blake." He smiles at us, then he turns and carries the baby down the hall. He's humming some kind of lullaby.

"God, babies are so gross," Madeleine says in a loud voice. I haven't heard her talk this much in two years. If Mr. Peterson can't hear her, he must be completely deaf. "Remember all those jokes about babies and their soft spots? I bet he'd break like an egg if you dropped him."

"Madeleine—will you please shut up?" Ellie hisses. She has two red circles on her cheeks. "You're not being funny. Dad can hear you."

"I don't care. I hate Dad, too. He's a fat butt-sniffer. I hope he drops that stupid baby." Madeleine's pulling on an earring in her left ear while she talks. She has a thousand holes in her ears. I wonder if that means she's in a gang. It could be a secret sign or something.

As usual, Madeleine's got on long sleeves, so I can't see her arms. Every time I see her, I wonder if her left arm's healed or if it still looks cut up and bruised. I know she can tell I'm watching her, too. Madeleine's one of those people who always knows what's going on with other people, even though she pretends she doesn't.

Maybe I should write an anonymous letter to the middle-school principal about her. I could sign it *A Concerned Friend.* I could say I've heard about a middle-school girls' gang that makes you poke holes in your ears and scratch up your arms before you can get in. The principal would probably have a nervous breakdown if I did that. People in this school district get extremely upset when anyone says there's a problem in one of the schools.

Madeleine pulls her hair down over her eyes, and her face disappears. "I need a haircut," she says to no one in particular. When she speaks, her hair moves. "I'm going to the bathroom to cut my hair right now. It's an emergency."

I hate to sound critical, but it's not a lot of fun to be around the Petersons these days. This is a pretty typical night, kind of like a very bad TV show. The trouble is, you know everything's not going to get better at the end of the show. Mrs. Peterson's always in hysterics about everything, and Madeleine looks like she wants to audition to be a member of the Addams Family, and Ellie—well, I don't even know how to describe Ellie. She just seems so sad all the time that it makes me feel terrible. I know that if I was a really good friend, like I'm supposed to be, that I'd be trying to make her feel better. That's what she'd do for me. But sometimes I can't. I start to feel worse and worse when I'm around her. Sometimes I think I'd rather go into a very deep coma than spend much time with Ellie because it's so depressing. That's an awful thing to think, I know. I hate myself when I think things like that. A truly good person would never have those thoughts.

"Did you girls see Blake?"

It's Misty. She's in a long, pink terry-cloth robe, and her hair's pulled back and pinned on top of her head.

She's very pretty, with blue eyes and soft skin, but she has dark circles around her eyes and she looks tired.

I think I know why. I hate to say it, but I'm pretty sure she and Mr. Peterson are having sex again. For a long time I thought that people their age didn't have sex, because they're so old. But Ellie said that Misty told her a few months ago that she and Mr. Peterson have sex frequently and it's always fabulous. She said that Misty knows a lot about sex, because she used to be a Dallas Cowboys cheerleader. I asked Ellie what Misty meant by *frequently*, and Ellie said at least once a week. Then I asked what Misty meant by *fabulous*, and Ellie said it was too revolting to talk about. Ellie doesn't like to talk about sex nearly as much as I do.

"I don't think they have sex anymore, since Misty got pregnant," Ellie said. "That's a big relief. I don't have to stuff cotton in my ears when I spend the night at their house. One time I heard them moaning, and it gave me nightmares for two weeks."

I was dying to ask what the moaning sounded like and how long it lasted, but I could tell Ellie didn't want to talk about it any longer. But now, since they've had their baby and Misty looks so tired, I'm pretty sure she and Mr. Peterson are having sex all the time again. I heard that sometimes people have sex so much that they forget to sleep. That doesn't sound

and sits down at the table. Everyone pretends not to notice that her hair's been cut off so that it's only about half an inch long. I think she may have shaved off her eyebrows, too, because I can't see them. She has a little cut on the left side of her forehead, and she's stuck a small piece of toilet paper on it. The blood's soaked through the paper and it looks very disgusting. Madeleine stares down at her plate and cuts the lasagna into little pieces with her fork. I think she's back in one of her nonverbal stages. Everyone starts talking more.

"Misty, you amaze me," Mr. Peterson says. "This lasagna is outstanding."

That's a very strange thing to say, since there are lots of white take-out containers in the kitchen, and I'm pretty sure the lasagna's from a gourmet-food place called Cook's Night Off on Oak Lawn. It's like making a big deal and asking for the recipe when someone opens a can of cream of mushroom soup and heats it up.

Mr. Peterson leans over and kisses Misty on the cheek, and she smiles back at him. Ellie and I say the lasagna's wonderful, too. Madeleine doesn't say anything. She's cutting up her lasagna in smaller and smaller pieces that look like specks on her plate, and I think she's frowning, but I'm not sure. It's hard to tell if someone's frowning when she doesn't have eyebrows anymore.

Misty smiles at us and then she begins to cry. "I'm just so happy," she says. She blows her nose into her napkin, and Mr. Peterson pats her shoulder. All of a sudden, you can hear the baby crying down the hall. Misty cries harder, and Mr. Peterson leans over and kisses her.

"You stay here, sweetheart," he says, "and I'll get the baby. Come on, girls, you can help me."

Ellie and I follow him. There's white, furry carpeting all the way down the hall. I hope I'm not tracking mud all over it.

Blake's nursery is at the end of the hall. It has striped blue-and-silver wallpaper, with blue footballs scattered all over it. The lamp is shaped like a silver helmet with a lightbulb on top. Blake's in a white baby bed in the corner, crying in a soft, high voice. Mr. Peterson leans over the bed and picks him up.

"Will you get a diaper out of the drawer, Ellie?" he asks. "They're in the right side of the bureau." He puts Blake on a white quilted blanket on top of a chest and unbuttons his tiny blue pajamas. Blake makes more soft, high cries and wiggles around a little bit in the lamp's white light. Mr. Peterson pulls his legs up gently and takes a sopping-wet diaper off. He pats

Blake's bottom with damp tissue and takes a new diaper from Ellie.

"This is so great," Mr. Peterson says. He looks at us and smiles. His eyes are wet and happy. "I just love being a father."

"He *what?*" Mrs. Peterson says. She slams on the brakes and stops the car in the middle of the street. She turns around to the backseat and glares at us. "What do you mean, your father is changing diapers, Ellie?"

Behind us, a horn honks. Mrs. Peterson lowers her window and gives the car behind us the finger. The other car whips around us loudly and honks again. You can see its back lights getting smaller in the distance.

"That son of a bitch never changed diapers for you and Madeleine. Not one diaper, ever. I changed every diaper myself, because your father was in law school and he couldn't be bothered. He was too good to change diapers when he was married to me."

"Mom," Ellie says, "it's not a big deal. I think he was just doing it because Misty was tired."

Mrs. Peterson turns back around. "Don't mention that slut's name in my new car." She hits the gas and the car roars off. It's some kind of Saab turbo, and it's really fast. Mrs. Peterson drives worse than most teenagers I know. "I let you girls go to dinner at your father's for just a few hours and what happens? Madeleine is totally unsupervised and she shaves off her hair in the bathroom—"

"I trimmed it," Madeleine says. She's sitting so far down in the front passenger seat that I can't see her head. "I couldn't find a razor in their stupid bathroom."

"—and my older daughter tells me that her father is now spending his life changing diapers. I just hope he doesn't forget to make a living, since he's so wrapped up in fatherhood. We're going to be dependent on him for child support until I find my new profession. But I don't feel guilty about taking money from your father. Oh, no. I earned that money—every penny of it. All those years I was married to that no-good—"

"Mom, please."

Mrs. Peterson stops talking and drives even faster. The car speeds along the street, and the white stripes of streetlights run across the dark leather seats. It's quiet inside the car till we pull into the driveway at Ellie's house. Mrs. Peterson turns off the ignition and then she starts to cry.

Ellie disappears into the house with her mother, and Madeleine and I follow a few minutes later. We're both walking very slowly so we don't catch up with Mrs. Peterson and Ellie. The minute we get inside the house, Madeleine runs up the stairs and slams her door. Then she starts playing some really horrible music. It sounds like a bunch of people who are locked up in an insane asylum, howling to get out. For someone who's supposed to be artistic, Madeleine has very bad taste in music.

I don't know what to do. I wander through the kitchen and try to clean it up a little bit. It's a big mess. There are dirty dishes everywhere and lots of overflowing ashtrays. The floor's supposed to be beige, but it's turned gray. Ellie told me that Carmelita quit this week. That's not exactly news. Carmelita quits at least once a month after she and Mrs. Peterson get into big fights over really stupid things, like what kind of dishwasher detergent to use. "Your mother is a fruitcake," she usually tells Ellie. "You understand what I'm sayin'? A real fruitcake."

"You know you don't really mean that, Carmelita," Ellie says.

That's the way people in the Peterson family communicate, as far as I can tell. They go around saying awful things to each other, and then the other person says he knows you don't mean it. But sometimes you do. Sometimes you mean everything you say, and it must be hard to hear that you don't, again and again. *You know that you don't mean that.* Well, what if I do?

One time, when Madeleine was in one of her verbal stages, I heard Mrs. Peterson pick at her for an hour or so. Nothing Madeleine did was right. She was stupid and slow and lazy and hateful. At the rate she was going, she would be a great big failure. Mrs. Peterson said she couldn't believe she'd wanted to have children. What a joke. Both her children—especially Madeleine—had just brought her heartbreak.

Finally Madeleine threw down everything she was working on and screamed at her mother. "I hate you!" she yelled. "Leave me alone! I hate you!"

I expected Mrs. Peterson to yell right back or start crying, but she didn't. She looked kind of pleased. "You know you don't mean that, Madeleine," she said. She was talking in a very quiet voice. "You're just upset."

For a minute she and Madeleine stared at each other. Mrs. Peterson looked perfectly calm, like she knew she'd just won something. What was it? I couldn't tell. Madeleine kicked at all the crayons and scissors and papers she'd been working with and scattered them all over the floor. Then she ran out of the room.

Mrs. Peterson shook her head and looked at Ellie and me. "That girl is so high-strung," she said. "I worry about her."

Ellie and I didn't say anything, but Mrs. Peterson kept looking at us. Something was happening, and I didn't know what it was, quite, but I knew Ellie did.

"Madeleine's a mess," Mrs. Peterson said. "That poor, poor girl. I blame your father, of course."

Ellie's eyes were on the ground.

"Don't you agree, Ellie?" Mrs. Peterson said.

For a minute Ellie didn't say anything.

Mrs. Peterson cleared her throat. "Ellie? Don't you agree, Ellie?"

Ellie's eyes were still on the ground, but she nodded. "Yes."

It's hard for me to explain what happened when Ellie said yes. It doesn't sound like much, but I knew it was important. Sometimes I still think about that scene—how something can look so small and insignificant but be so important that you remember it forever—even if you still don't understand what it means, exactly.

I scrape a few dishes and put them in the dishwasher, but the kitchen still looks horrible. I hope Carmelita comes back soon. I don't think Mrs. Peterson can do anything by herself. She gets very tired a lot of the time. That's what Ellie's always telling me.

Sometimes I wonder what grown-ups like Mrs. Peterson and Mr. Peterson used to be like before they got old. I wonder if you could look at them then and tell what's going to happen to them and how they're going to change. I don't think you can, though. You can see pictures of them when they were younger—like those pictures of Mrs. Peterson in the living room. But they don't tell you enough. They just get you started, and you know you're missing a thousand other things you'll never find out about. That's the trouble with trying to understand people, I think. You never know enough.

One time Mrs. Peterson told Ellie and me that when she was in high school and college, it was the happiest time of her life. She kept on talking for a long, long time. Mrs. Peterson really talks a lot when she's not depressed. She told us about all her boyfriends and her sorority and how she never had time to study because she was so popular. I didn't listen to her that closely, so I don't remember everything she said. The only thing I really remember was when she told us that she thought she'd be that happy for the rest of her life.

"My life was wonderful then. It was amazing," she said. "I guess I thought it would always be like that."

Mrs. Peterson smiled for a few seconds after she said that. Then she stopped talking and her face changed. I've never forgotten how it looked. Her face looked like it had been squeezed hard and all the life in it was gone.

It was the first time I'd ever really looked at Mrs. Peterson. And then I wished I hadn't, because I felt like I was seeing too much. I could tell from her face that she knew she'd lost everything and it was never coming back. Her face was sad and quiet, and for a few minutes she didn't even move.

7 seven

It's the second week of November, and it's supposed to be ninety-one degrees tomorrow afternoon. Mom and I watch the ten o'clock news and all the newspeople do is joke about how it's so hot, you can fry an egg on the sidewalk, but no one fries eggs any longer because of the cholesterol.

"My God," Mom says. "Is that supposed to be clever?" She grabs the remote control and turns off the TV.

She's in a very bad mood today. I think it's because she just opened an envelope from Nana, and it was full of newspaper articles. Nana mails her lots of articles about teenage girls and how their lives are in danger. Nana keeps track of all the ways you can die when you're my age. She says that shows how much she loves me. When she sends the articles to Mom, she marks them with a yellow highlighter so Mom won't miss any important points. Today she sent a clipping with the headline *Warning: Mothers Who Work May Be Harming Their Children's Health.* Nana smeared yellow highlighter all over the headline and added three exclamation marks to it.

As usual, Mom looked at Nana's letter while she was standing over a trash can and let it drop in. She didn't say anything. She almost never talks about Nana. One time she told me that she was very nervous about having a daughter because her relationship with Nana was so awful. For a minute I thought that Mom was going to ask me what I thought about our relationship. But she didn't, and I was glad. I wouldn't have known what to say to her. We've never been close, and I don't know why. I guess we just have different personalities.

Sometimes I want to talk to Mom, but I don't know how and neither does she. One time I heard someone in the hall say that her mother was her best friend, and I got so upset I almost ran into the wall. I felt like I couldn't breathe. I wondered what it would be like to have a mother you could talk to about anything. Or to have your mother think you're interesting. It must be great.

For a long time after Dad died, I could tell Mom was trying to be extra nice to me. She took me shopping and we went to the movies—you know, all those things you can do with someone so you don't have to talk. When we were together, she touched me more than she used to. Sometimes she hugged and kissed me. I guess she felt like she had to do that, since Dad had just died.

I felt awful then. I felt so sad that I wanted to die. But I knew I had to keep moving so I'd feel better. Sometimes when we'd stop to get a Coke, I'd look at Mom's face when she wasn't noticing me. She looked sad, and I could see a line that ran from her mouth past her chin. I'd never seen that line before.

I knew that Mom felt bad about Dad's death, but it was just like the divorce. We didn't know how to talk to each other about anything important. So she smiled at me and then I smiled back, and we talked about the ice-skaters on the rink below us. I was so cold, sitting there by the ice-skating rink in the shopping mall.

Mom and I sat there and stared at the figures going around the ice rink and listened to the sound of skates cutting ice. It looked like we were together, but we weren't. We'd never done anything together, really. We'd just pretended to.

I always loved Dad more than Mom. That sounds terrible to say, but it's true and I can't help it. That's something both Mom and I know. It's one of those things we know but we never talk about.

Sometimes it's almost like a picture I can see in my mind. There's Dad in the middle, and Mom and I are on either side of him. Even after Mom and Dad got divorced and I lived with Mom, Dad was still in the middle. He was the one I always talked to, not Mom. Mom talked to him about me. And then he talked to us about each other. We needed him in between us.

I think the picture was always like that, even when I was a little kid. Dad was there, right between me and Mom. Lots of time passed and we got older and things changed, but our picture never did. Even when Dad died, Mom and I still stood the way we always had. We're both staring straight ahead, looking at something else. It's like we're frozen, and there will always be something between us, even if no one else can see it. Dad's gone, but we're still saving his place for him.

Today's been a wonderful day! I mean it–*wonderful!* I think it's the high point of my life so far.

In world history Coach Morrison gets called to the principal's office right in the middle of class. He tells us we can have a study hall while he's gone. That's when Ben and I start talking. We talk for *twenty-six minutes*. I'm sure about that, because I'm timing it. When the bell rings, I realize that I'm definitely sure that I'm passionately in love with Ben. Completely and totally, head over heels in love. I've never felt like this before.

I think about Ben the rest of the day. Every few minutes I look up and see my teachers talking, but I can't hear anything. It's like watching a silent movie. Sometimes I try to hear what they're saying, but it's too much work. I feel like I'm floating out of the room on a big cloud instead. I'm relieved when school's finally out and none of my teachers have noticed that I have absolutely no idea what they've been talking about.

When I get home from school, there are two messages on our voice mail. One's from Nana. She wants to make sure we don't miss a TV special on divorce tonight. It's called "Broken Homes, Broken Lives," she says. Peter Jennings is narrating it, and she thinks he's very good, even though someone told her he was from Canada.

The next is from Ellie. "Where were you, Sarah? I waited by my locker for fifteen minutes and you didn't show up. You were supposed to come over here, remember? Call me. Bye."

I dial Ellie's number, but no one answers. I leave a message about how I'm sorry I forgot I was supposed to meet her. I listen to my voice while I say that, and I know I don't sound sorry. I don't feel sorry, either, and that makes me feel bad. The truth is, I'm glad Ellie didn't answer the phone. I don't like to talk to her all the time the way I used to. Sometimes I think she and I are getting more and more different but we're pretending like we're not.

Besides, Ellie wouldn't want to hear about what a great day I had today. She doesn't like to talk about anything that happens at school or being in love or anything like that. And that's what I want to think about right now.

This is the first time I've ever been in love, and I want to be by myself so I can think about Ben. Maybe if Ellie calls back, I can tell her about it, but I don't think she'll understand. She's never been in love before, and it's hard to explain what it feels like.

The downstairs door bangs and I can hear Mom. I tell her I'll be down soon, but I don't move. I sit on my bed and stare out the window. I think about talking to Ben, and how I noticed for the first time that he has the most beautiful eyes I've ever seen in my life. They're such a dark green that they're almost brown. They also look very deep, like you could jump into them and stay there forever.

I wish I could talk about this to Mom, but I know I can't. Mom doesn't have very many emotions—that's the problem. She doesn't have emotions and I have too many. That's why we can't understand each other. I've never seen Mom cry once, not even at Dad's funeral, and sometimes I think it would help if I saw her cry about something. But she's not the kind of person who cries. She's too strong. I'm the only one in our house who cries, and I try to be very quiet about it. I cry every time someone hurts my feelings, and my feelings get hurt about twenty-five times a day. I know that's immature and I need to stop it. But it's hard.

I can hear voices downstairs. Mom must be here with her boyfriend. His name is Joe, and he's a county judge.

I know I'm supposed to hate anyone my parents date, but I like Joe. When I first met him in February, I tried to hate him, but I finally gave up because it was too much work. The trouble is, he's very nice and funny. He's tall and thin, and he's got a bald spot right on top of his head that he's always trying to cover up. He's divorced and he doesn't have any kids, but I can tell he likes them, since he's very nice to me. Besides, it's more fun to be around Mom when Joe's here. She's been a lot happier since they started going out.

I don't want to sound disgusting, but I think that Mom and Joe are having sex, just like Misty and Mr. Peterson. I figured that out last summer. It happened when Mom and I were watching a video called *Bull Durham*. That's a very embarrassing movie to watch with your mother, because the man and woman were pretty old, and once they started having sex they couldn't stop. One time they had sex on the kitchen table, and there wasn't even a tablecloth on it.

When the movie was over, Mom had a funny look on her face, kind of like a smile. She asked me if I knew everything I needed to know about sex. I said yes, I knew everything, even though I was dying to ask if most grown-ups had sex on the kitchen table. Mom's face was a little redder than usual and she kept smiling and she seemed to be in a good mood. That was when I figured out that she and Joe were probably sleeping together. She didn't used to look nearly as happy when she talked to me about sex. In fact, one time she told me that sex wasn't that big a deal, even though everybody thought it was. But the way she looked when she was talking to me last summer, I could tell she'd changed her mind.

I go downstairs, and Joe and Mom are in the kitchen, opening a bottle of wine. Joe's not like my father at all. He's very quiet. Sometimes when I watch him, I can see how nervous he is. I think he's in love with Mom. When you're in love yourself, then you can recognize other people who are in love, too. I read that somewhere.

When I walk in the room, Mom and Joe are looking at each other. There's something so strong that passes between the two of them that I can almost see it. It's there for a moment, then it's gone.

Mom gives her head a little shake and reaches her hand toward me. "Sarah," she says. "I'm sorry I was so late. How are you? What happened today?"

She and Joe turn to look at me. They both smile,

and for a moment I think about how I am and what happened today.

I'm in love, I think. *I'm in love with Ben Cooper, but he doesn't know it.*

I need to go to a therapist because I think about sex all the time.

I don't like my best friend as much as I used to, and that makes me feel terrible.

I think I failed an algebra test because I didn't study enough.

I miss Dad. I think about him every day. I feel like someone's squeezing my heart when I think about him. But I can't say anything to you or anybody else. Nobody wants me to talk about him.

All of a sudden, all my happiness drains out. I feel so lonely that I want to cry. I don't know why. I don't know why I ever thought I was happy in the first place.

I open my mouth to talk, but I can't say anything. I know I should stay and talk to Mom and Joe and try to have fun with them. But I just don't feel like it tonight. Just thinking about trying to be funny and smart makes me feel tired and sad.

They're trying to be nice to me, I know. But I wish they wouldn't try so hard. I make myself smile and then I move toward the door.

"I've got a lot more homework," I say. "I just came in to say hello."

* * *

It's 5 A.M. now, and I still haven't gotten to sleep. It's very unhealthy when you don't get enough sleep. It might stunt my growth. I want to be five-ten when I grow up, but I'm only five-three now. I try to stretch a lot so I'll grow more, but I don't think it helps.

Nana says I'm not any taller because Mom doesn't feed me well. She says that Mom is too wrapped up in her career to take care of her only child. Nana's a member of a group called Concerned Women of America, and she gives me a lot of things they send her. One of the bulletins last month said that working women were the greatest danger to this country since fluoride in the drinking water. That's why the Communists invented women's liberation, Nana says—so they could break up the American family. Sometimes I tell Nana that the cold war is over and there aren't Communists around any longer, but it doesn't do any good. Nana says the Communists are just pretending to be gone and she's not going to let them fool her. They're very tricky people, she says.

I turn my pillow over. Maybe that will help me get back to sleep. Not getting enough sleep can also give you pimples. All I need is more pimples. It's hard to have a good personality when you have big pimples on your face. Ben is never going to fall in love with me if I get acne and then I have to wear a veil over my face.

When they talk to you, adults always try to act like the way you look isn't important. Have you noticed that? They love to tell you things like how it's more important to have substance than beauty. I don't know why they say things like that when they're not true.

Last summer I was watching a lot of TV, and one afternoon I saw a talk show about three women from different parts of the country and how they were proud they'd kept their harelips. I'd never seen anyone with a harelip before. I made myself stare at their faces so I'd be prepared if I ever saw someone like them in real life and I could act very casual and I wouldn't have a heart attack or anything. Two of them had kind of lopsided faces, and they all wore bright red lipstick.

Every time they were in front of the camera, the three women smiled a lot and patted their hair and tried to act like they were really happy about their faces. But the more they smiled and laughed, the sadder I got. They reminded me of Mrs. Peterson when she's taking up a new hobby or believing in crystals or going to treadmill aerobics classes and she tells Ellie and me that she's finally found something that's going to change her life forever and make her a new person. She has the same kind of look on her face as those women. She always smiles, and if you didn't know her, you'd think she was happy and she was going to be fine. I'd seen her look like that so many times and it made me want to cry, because I knew it wouldn't last, and after it was over she was going to feel worse than she did before. That's what made me so sad about these three women. It wasn't their harelips, really. It was the fact they were trying too hard to look happy.

I guess I was the only one who felt that way, though. The studio audience gave the three women a standing ovation after the woman from Oregon said, "I'm not disfigured. I have a distinctive face. I have a face people remember."

The three of them stood together on the stage, holding hands, and then they raised their hands together and everybody applauded even harder. The host of the show, a blond woman named Nanette who had green glasses that matched her suit, came running up on the stage. She said these women were her heroes, because they had been empowered by their facial flaws. They all hugged each other, kind of like a huddle in a football game, and everyone applauded even more.

All the credits were running and Nanette and the three women with the harelips were all crying and smiling. I'm sure everybody else thought it was very inspiring and thrilling, but I felt so awful about it, I wanted to die. I kept wondering what would happen when the show was over and the cameras were turned off and the audience left. That's what happens when you have a mother who works in TV. You think about those things. I was pretty sure that those women would go back to their homes and they'd never see each other again and Nanette would forget all about them. I knew they were feeling great right now, but I knew they'd feel a lot worse next week. I don't know why I knew that, but I did.

It always seemed sad to me when people went around insisting that things like beauty and dates and popularity didn't matter when they knew it wasn't true. Why couldn't they just admit that things like that did matter and that life was sad and unfair sometimes and that maybe if you cried a lot about it, then you'd feel better later? Why do they have to go around lying about things like this?

eight

Ms. Evans is back in our English class. She hadn't said anything about Miss Lester, who was the substitute teacher while she was gone. Every afternoon I've gone through the newspapers looking for a story about Miss Lester. I was afraid that she jumped off a flagpole or something after she taught our class. But I haven't read anything. Maybe they haven't found her body yet. That must be it. She killed herself in some very quiet way, and her body hasn't even been found. That would be terrible. If you're going to kill yourself, it would be nice to make other people feel guilty at least. Not that I think anyone like Robert or Alex would ever feel guilty about anything. They don't have much of a conscience.

Today we talk about a short story we just read called "The Lady or the Tiger?" It's about a woman who has to choose between having the guy she loves marry another woman or get killed by a tiger. I read the story last night and I tried to imagine what I'd do. I thought about Ben and Emily Reif and how Emily's like an evil goddess. I decided that Ben would be better off with the tiger. A lot better off.

"So—what did you think of the short story?" Ms. Evans asks. I like her, even though she gave me that bad grade last week. "Which do you think she chose, the lady or the tiger?"

Three or four of the boys raise their hands, and they all say they're sure she chose the lady. "The chick's behind door number one," Alex Baxter says. He grins at Ms. Evans, but she doesn't smile back. If I were Alex, I'd stop talking.

"Definitely the chick," Alex says again. The other boys hoot and make a lot of noise and claps.

"Girls?" Ms. Evans says. "Don't you have opinions?"

She's always pushing us to speak up. She says if we don't watch it, the boys will take over the class. That's why there's never been a woman president, Ms. Evans says. "Cut out the passive stuff and tell me what you think," she tells us sometimes. But I almost never say anything. Neither do most of the other girls.

"Girls?" she says again, in a louder voice. "Do I have to call on one of you?" No one says anything. "Lauren—what do you think?"

Lauren Jensen turns bright red. She looks like she wants to die. She's one of those people who goes to church three times a week, and she's even quieter than I am.

"The chick, the chick," Alex chants. "Pick the chick."

"Lauren?" Ms. Evans says again.

Lauren clears her throat. "Well ..." Her voice trails off. Then she sits up straighter. "I know this doesn't sound very Christian, but I think it's the tiger. That's what I'd do if it was my boyfriend."

Alex stops chanting and stares at Lauren like she's grown a horn between her eyes. He looks confused. "Huh?" he says.

"Anyone else?" Ms. Evans asks.

For a few seconds it's quiet. Then all the girls start talking. We all raise our hands and shake them back and forth and vote for the tiger.

"Meow!" someone says.

"Behind door number one—the tiger!"

We start to giggle and laugh. I'm laughing so hard that my stomach hurts and tears roll down my face. Even Ms. Evans is laughing. But the boys don't say anything. Not one word. I've been going to school with Alex Baxter since we were in kindergarten and this is the first time I can remember him being completely silent.

The bell rings. The boys don't move. But all of us girls walk out in the hall together. We're still screeching with laughter and making so much noise that everyone turns around and stares at us.

"Did you see Alex Baxter's face?" Stephanie Rider

asks me. She's a tall girl with long black hair. "He looked like he just swallowed a football."

She and I walk down the hall together. Every few steps we start laughing again. I don't think I've ever laughed this hard in my life.

"See you," Stephanie says as she turns the corner. She gives me a brief wave and I wave back.

Later that morning I run into Ellie in the hall. She's holding her books so tight that her knuckles are almost white. Her eyes are red, and I'm pretty sure she must have been crying.

"What's wrong?" I ask. "Is it your mom again?"

She shakes her head slowly, back and forth. "It's Madeleine. She ran away yesterday. It was awful. We thought somebody had kidnapped her."

"But she's okay?"

"Yeah. She's okay." Ellie exhales a long breath that sounds more like a sob. I hope she doesn't start crying right now. I don't think you should cry in public, especially when you're at school. It's too embarrassing. If you have to cry, I think you should go to the girls' rest room and lock yourself in a stall. That's what I always do.

Ellie looks up at me. Her eyes are wet and a tear rolls down her cheek.

I need to help her. I know that. But everything in

me leans back, away from her. I want to leave, but I don't. But I don't do anything else, either. I don't tell Ellie that I'll be there when she needs me. I don't offer to come over to her house. I don't do anything.

In the background I can hear the bell ringing. I'm so happy to hear that bell, it's ridiculous.

"We're going to be late to class," I say.

"Yes," Ellie says. She's looking down at the ground again. "Yes, I know that."

Her voice sounds lower than it used to be. It sounds so sad and lonely that I want to die.

I rush to my next class and all I can hear are the sounds of people laughing and talking. They're happy sounds. Sometimes that's what I want to hear—happy sounds. I don't want to hear anything else.

Do you know what I mean? I've been sad for so long that it's nice to laugh for a change.

That night I can't get to sleep. I lie there in the dark and think about Ellie and how sad she was today. I know I should have helped her. I know I should have done something. But I just couldn't. All I wanted to do was run away and keep running. I want to run away from Ellie and I want to run away from everything I remember about Dad. I want to run away and be someone who's lighter and freer, just for a while. I don't want to feel sad all the time. I'm sick of it.

I turn over and over in bed, and finally I fall asleep. When I wake up, it's three in the morning. It's always three when I wake up. I don't know why.

For once I remember what I was dreaming about. It was the last trip I made with Dad and it happened a year ago. I keep thinking about everything that happened a year ago. It's like I have to go back and relive the worst time of my life over and over. I don't know why. Living through something once is hard enough. Why should you have to go back?

I still have the dream's pictures in my mind. I was dreaming about the horizon in West Texas. It's broad and flat and it makes you feel small, because it's so gigantic. Some people don't like it. They say it's empty and boring and ugly. But I loved it, because Dad did. Dad always said he loved West Texas because it was open and it made him feel free and more alive, just being there. "These are my roots, darlin'," he said once. "My roots." He pronounced *roots* like a West Texan, with a vowel sound like *good.*

Dad was visiting oil fields on that trip. He and I drove west through Arlington, past baseball fields and roller coasters and a wax museum, and through the middle of downtown Fort Worth, where the traffic slowed to a stop. Dad had a thermos beside him and he sipped black coffee and fiddled with the radio dial until he found a country-and-western station.

I told him I didn't know how anybody could drink coffee without milk or sugar in it. I also said I didn't know how anybody but a moron could listen to country-and-western music.

"That's because your heart's never been broke, darlin'," he said. "Minute that happens, you'll listen to country-and-western music all the time. It's the best thing on God's green earth—next to a bar—when you're drownin' in self-pity."

Dad never really cared about grammar. But the way he talked always got worse when we headed out of town. Once you couldn't see the skyscrapers anymore, he started talking like Willie Nelson or somebody. I think it was because he was trying to prove he didn't put on airs. Dad was from a small town in West Texas called Big Spring. He said that by the time he realized *ain't* wasn't a word, he was already a millionaire and he'd be damned if he was going to change his language. I think that was an exaggeration.

When we were finally out of the city traffic and off the interstate, Dad pulled back in his seat and stretched his arms and legs. He was wearing a plaid shirt and blue jeans and boots that day. I can still see them when I close my eyes. I can still see him and I can still smell him—that mixture of bourbon and cigars that always makes me feel happy and safe.

Outside, it was misty and cold, and the land was

flat and brown. We were the only people on the road. The yellow line in the middle of the highway seemed like it stretched on forever, till it got lost in the mist. Dad pressed the gas down and started going even faster. He always said that his idea of perfect freedom was to drive as fast as he could and drink beer and roll down the windows and let the hot air blow through and listen to Hank Williams songs till his ears bled.

I took a nap for a while, and when I woke up, Dad was pulling into a gravel parking lot with three pickup trucks and a weather-beaten Suburban in it. We're at a café called The Bluebonnet, and Dad and I always stopped there for cheeseburgers in waxed paper and real cherry Cokes. The café has yellow venetian blinds and booths with Formica tops and, right above the cash register, there's a deer's head with big black eyes. Under the deer's head there's a sign that says, *This deer bounced a check—and look what happened to him.*

A waitress who was about Nana's age took our order and stuck her pencil into the curly gray hair behind her ear. "Be right back with your orders, hon," she said. She was like everybody else in the café, with a lined, sunburned face. Even though Dad had on his jeans and boots, he and I looked different from everyone else. We looked like city slickers, but I wasn't sure why. I loved coming here, but I didn't feel like I belonged. I don't think Dad did, either.

After we left the café, Dad and I pulled into a filling station. Dad stood by the car and talked to the attendant in bad Spanish. He probably had the worst Spanish accent I ever heard in my life, and most of the time he just put *el* in front of an English word and added an *o* to the end. The filling-station worker wore a red baseball hat and had his name, Philberto, sewn on his front shirt pocket. He seemed very happy to talk to Dad, even though you could tell he didn't understand a lot of what Dad was trying to say. Everybody always liked to talk to Dad. He made people happy. There was just something about him that I can't explain.

The next morning Dad and I stopped at an oil rig. I stayed inside a small house on the property and stared out the windows and watched the wind blow. The sky was reddish brown, and sheets of dust swept past. Every time the wind blew hard, the house shook a little. I looked outside and didn't see anyone. I felt like I was the only person left on earth.

When I was younger, Dad used to tell me a story about the wife of a rancher who lived in the Panhandle, in the north part of Texas. Her husband traveled for days and weeks and left her alone in their house. Some days she got so lonely, she talked to her chickens.

For some reason, I've never forgotten that story. I think about it every time I come to West Texas. I don't think I'd be a very good pioneer. I don't think I'm tough enough. I don't even like to go camping, for one thing.

After his meeting was over, Dad and I drove to a rest home about forty miles away to see one of his aunts. The home's in a town called Anson. Anson is sort of famous because for years they wouldn't allow dancing there. That's because there were so many Southern Baptists and Church of Christers in the town. If you go to the Church of Christ, you can't even have an organ in your church, because organs aren't mentioned in the Bible. Dancing is even worse. Everyone goes around telling jokes about Southern Baptists and Church of Christers and how they can never have sexual intercourse standing up, because someone might think they're dancing. I was very interested the first time I heard that joke because I hadn't realized you could have sex standing up. I bet it makes you dizzy.

The rest home was called Oakwood Trails. It was very depressing. Dad and I walked down the long, dark halls, and every time we passed a door I looked in and saw someone lying in a bed. Sometimes we could hear people moaning and screaming. It even smelled depressing, kind of musty and sad and old.

Dad talked to one of the nurses behind a desk. Then he led me down the hall. The door was partly open. The room was small and even darker than the hall. A hospital bed was pushed up against the wall, and there was a woman lying there with her head tilted up on a pillow. She was Dad's aunt Dorothy. I could remember seeing her every year when I was younger. She loved children and she always gave me peppermint candies wrapped in clear paper. For someone who was so old, she was pretty much fun. She wore dresses in bright colors with lots of flowers on them, and she always had two spots of red on her cheeks where she put on makeup and forgot to cover it up. She laughed a lot, too.

"Aunt Dottie," Dad said. He got a chair and pulled it up to the side of her bed and took one of her hands.

Aunt Dottie looked at him for a second. Then she stared up at the ceiling again. She used to be plump and wear lots of perfume. But that day, she looked tiny under her blanket. Her hair was all gray and her mouth kept moving, opening and closing. Her eyes were empty.

"Aunt Dottie," Dad said again. "It's Tommy—remember? Your favorite nephew. And look who I've brought with me this time. It's my daughter, Sarah."

He motioned for me to come closer to the bed.

I wished he wouldn't do that. "Sarah's changed so much, Aunt Dottie. She's a young lady now. I bet you won't even recognize her."

I didn't move for a few seconds. Dad gestured impatiently, and I finally edged closer to the bed. I didn't want to see Aunt Dottie like this. I wanted to remember her the way she used to be, when she laughed and burned roast beef in the oven and tried to sing like Patsy Cline when the radio was on. I didn't want to be there. It was too sad.

"It's Sarah, Aunt Dottie," Dad said. "Sarah."

Aunt Dottie's eyes turned to me. They were a different color than they used to be, a lighter blue. She opened and closed her mouth again and then she started to moan. It was the first sound she'd made since we got there. Her eyes were sad and scared and blank, all at the same time. Every time she opened her mouth, she moaned louder.

Dad still had his hand covering hers. He leaned his head over and kissed her hand. For a few seconds, he didn't move. He just sat there, with his head over her hand. When he finally raised his head, his cheeks were wet. I'd never seen Dad cry before. I know this sounds terrible, but it always seems worse and sadder to me when a man cries. I think it's because you can tell they haven't had any practice at it and they don't know what to do or what kinds of noises to make. I know that sounds very sexist, but I can't help it. Seeing Dad cry made me feel lonely and scared.

Aunt Dottie looked at his face. Then she moaned louder. She stared up at the ceiling and moved around in her bed. She made louder noises and gasps, then she began to scream. I felt like her screams were filling up the room and I couldn't breathe anymore. I needed to get out. I wanted to run away and jump in the car and drive away as fast as I could. I didn't want to be there. I was afraid I was going crazy. I had to leave.

"Dad—we have to go."

Dad put his hand on my shoulder and squeezed it. He didn't move. Aunt Dottie screamed again and again.

"Dad—she doesn't know who we are. We're upsetting her. Maybe if we go, she'll calm down."

Dad rose slowly out of the chair. He didn't usually move that slowly. He and I left Aunt Dottie's room and walked down the hall, past all the rooms with people in their beds, waiting to die. Even the TV was turned off when we walked past the lounge. It was quiet, except for Aunt Dottie's screams.

We walked past the nurses' station, and the nurse Dad had talked to earlier called out to us. "Did you find your aunt?"

Dad nodded, but he didn't say anything.

The nurse looked at both of us. She had friendly

brown eyes and a smile that seemed warm and sad. She shook her head and sighed. "Mrs. Palmer hasn't known anyone in a long time," she said. "It's been months. It's always a shock the first time you see them when they're like that."

Dad pulled a tissue out of the container at the nurses' station and blew his nose loudly, like some kind of broken foghorn. Then he took off his glasses and wiped his eyes and blew his nose again, even more loudly. It was kind of reassuring to hear him make so much noise. It made me think everything was back to normal.

"Goddamn, life's sad sometimes," Dad said. "Breaks your heart, don't it?"

I couldn't tell who he was talking to. But the nurse and I both nodded.

After we left Anson, Dad and I drove back to Dallas. I can remember looking out the window, watching the sun come in and out of the clouds. Just when I got used to it, it changed. I put my feet on the dashboard and stared up through the moonroof and watched the clouds and patches of blue sky. I thought about the last time I saw Aunt Dottie. It was two years ago at Thanksgiving. She came to Dallas and stayed with Dad, and you could already tell there was something wrong with her. She walked very slowly, and when she sat down she hunched over. The only things that moved were her hands. Her right hand kept gripping her skirt and then letting it go. Then it rubbed against her left hand. Then she rubbed her hands together. She did that again and again, and I wondered why. I didn't know if she knew what she was doing or if it made her feel better.

She talked to me a little and told me about Dad when he was a little boy. She and her husband, Frank, had lived across the alley from Dad's family. Most nights Dad had dinner with them. She and Frank hadn't had any children, and Dad was just like their very own son, she told me.

"Tommy was a real firecracker," she said. "Smart and sassy. I think he was too much for his parents. He ever tell you about the time he snuck that sugar in the sheriff's gas tank?" She grinned at me and we both laughed. That was one of the famous stories from Dad's childhood, along with the time he set the neighbor's roof on fire.

I loved Aunt Dottie. For an old woman, she was a lot of fun. I wished Nana was more like her. Sometimes when I looked at Aunt Dottie's face, I could see Dad, even if she wasn't his mother. There was something about them that was exactly alike.

Five minutes later Aunt Dottie told me the same story about Dad again. "Your daddy," she said, "was a real firecracker." She probably told that story a hundred times over Thanksgiving, the same way she kept moving her hands together. When she started the story, everyone would stop talking and eating and would listen again and again and laugh in all the right places. It was like there were just a few things in her mind, and she was going over the stories she loved over and over. I guess it made her happy every time she did.

So maybe Aunt Dottie had been happy two years ago. I knew it made Dad and me and all of Dad's cousins feel bad to hear her repeat herself and see how slowly she moved—but at least she seemed happy. She wasn't the same as she had been, but at least she was still there, off and on.

But now she was gone. You could look in her eyes and all you saw was some kind of emptiness. There wasn't any light. Aunt Dottie was alive, but she wasn't there any longer, not really. I wondered what had happened. I wondered if there had been any one, certain moment when she had been there for a few seconds, smiling and laughing and telling the same story—and then she was gone. When had that happened? Was anybody there to notice? Had she realized what was happening?

I hated thinking about things like this because it

made me so sad. Sometimes I wished I was religious, because I might have felt happier if I thought everyone was going to live forever in heaven. But I didn't believe that, and maybe it wouldn't have helped, anyway. Because Aunt Dottie hadn't been dead—so how could her soul be in heaven? It must have been trapped inside her, trying to get out. That was why she'd moaned and screamed. In a way, it was worse than being dead.

The miles raced by, but Dad and I didn't talk. He didn't even have the radio on for once. We passed through Sweetwater, which is where Dad almost always got speeding tickets and then griped and complained about it for the rest of the trip. Every year they have a Rattlesnake Roundup in Sweetwater, and all the animal-rights people get very upset about it. Two years ago a bunch of protesters showed up, and they had signs that said things like *Give the Rattlesnake a Fair Shake.* One of them tried to let a bunch of rattlesnakes loose and he got bitten on the big toe by one of them. People in Sweetwater are still laughing about that.

The light got dimmer and dimmer, and pretty soon the only thing I could see in the car was the glow of numbers and gauges behind the steering wheel. Sometimes Dad would roll down the window and throw out an empty beer can. Dad loved to throw beer cans out the window. I used to tell him not to litter, but I finally gave up. That's the way he was.

That was just the way he was. That's what I always thought about Dad. He was the way he was, and you could never change him. He shouldn't have driven as fast as he did. He shouldn't have drunk as much or smoked cigars. He shouldn't have spent so much money. He should have been a more moderate person, that's what Mom says. He would have lived longer—a lot longer—if he had been. But he wouldn't have been Dad if he'd done that. He might have lived longer, but he would have been someone else.

Driving into the edge of Fort Worth, we passed road signs and billboards and strip shopping malls. Between Fort Worth and Dallas the traffic got heavier and heavier, and you could see the downtown skyline in the distance.

When I think about that time now, I know something was wrong. But I didn't know it then. Thinking back, I can feel some kind of sadness that was there with us, but I just wasn't aware of it. I knew something was wrong. I knew there was something different about Dad. It was like he was almost haunted by something, and that made him drive faster and drink even more.

But I never would have asked him about it. That

was never the way he and I were together. We talked about my problems and we talked about life and politics and sports and we joked and laughed. But we never talked about anything that might be bothering Dad, because he wasn't that kind of person. He was the kind of person who could handle anything, who could make everything all right.

So that's why I just sat there and watched the billboards and freeway signs flash into view and then disappear. I was staring straight ahead, daydreaming, and even though we were back in the city, I still thought the horizon stretched on forever.

nine

"Why don't you come over to my house?" Stephanie asks after school one day. She's the tall girl in my English class. "We could do our homework and talk."

I've never been to Stephanie's house before. It's been a long time since I've been to anyone but Ellie's house. I call and leave a message for Mom on her voice mail at work and tell her where I'll be.

I hope I don't see Ellie when we leave the school. I haven't been to her house in two weeks. I haven't felt like it. I told her I've been working on a science project all the time after school, and that's why I couldn't come to her house. That's a big lie. I haven't even started my science project. I don't think Ellie believed me, but she acted like she did. That made me feel even worse. If she'd gotten angry at me, I would have felt better.

Stephanie's mother picks us up in a long, sleek green car. I think it's a Jaguar. She has short brown hair and freckles, and she's wearing a sweatsuit that says *Ski New Mexico,* with a drawing of a jalapeño pepper skiing down a mountain.

"I'm a big fan of your mother's," she says when Stephanie introduces me. "I bet you eat well at home."

That's what everybody says to me, but it isn't true. The truth is, Mom and I eat a lot of pizza and frozen foods and leftovers from her show. Lots of times when she gets home, Mom's so sick of cooking and tasting things that she doesn't want to do anything at all. Besides, she can't enjoy herself while she's cooking. She says it used to be a lot more fun when it was still a hobby.

"Uh-huh," I say. Mom hates answers like that. She says they're Neanderthal and inarticulate, but I don't care. I love noncommittal answers. *Uh-huh, I don't eat well. Uh-huh, my life isn't like you think it is. Uh-huh, I'm not a big fan of my mother's.*

"I'll drop you girls off, then I'm going to the gym," Mrs. Rider says into the rearview mirror. "Scott's got a soccer game at five. We're supposed to bring drinks."

Stephanie fluffs her hair back and yawns loudly. "Wonderful. I just *love* watching midgets playing soccer." Scott's her twelve-year-old brother, she tells me later. She's pretty sure he's retarded, but she doesn't think her parents have noticed yet. "Or his teachers, either," she says. "He's very smart, for a retarded kid."

Stephanie's house is old and big, with a broad front porch and stained-glass windows in the entryway. She and I sit in the kitchen and eat a whole box of frozen

Girl Scout thin-mint cookies. We talk about Alex's Halloween party. Stephanie says that a Deep Ellum band called the Yeast Infections played at the party, and Emily Reif got so drunk that she vomited all over the dance floor. She also says she thinks Alex might go completely insane and have to be institutionalized because he masturbates so much. Her great-aunt gave her a book called *That Special Time of Your Life,* and it says that boys who masturbate a lot have yellow eyes, just like Alex's.

"Plus they're nearsighted," Stephanie says, crunching another cookie. "They masturbate and they don't wash their hands before they touch their eyes, and their eyes just shrivel up overnight. I once heard Alex say he was very nearsighted." Stephanie pauses and wipes her face off with a napkin. "He might go blind pretty soon."

Stephanie says she knows a lot more about sex than most freshmen because her father's a Christian psychiatrist. "He believes in a healthy sex life after you're married. He says it's God's will for all of us to have sex a lot, and every time you have normal intercourse with your spouse it makes God and all the angels very happy."

She shrugs. "My mom's got some red crotchless panties with black lace. They're revolting. Do you want to see them? One time I told my dad I didn't think red crotchless panties were in the Bible. He said he doesn't believe in a literal translation of the Bible and sometimes you have to read between the lines. He said when I get older, I can read the Song of Solomon, and I'll see where red crotchless panties would fit in just fine. Then he told me to stop sneaking around, looking in other people's drawers. What do you think?"

"About what?"

Stephanie's parents sound kind of perverted to me. I've never heard anybody else say you're supposed to have as much sex as possible so you can go to heaven. No wonder Mrs. Rider looked so peppy. I don't think religion's supposed to be that much fun. But maybe that's because I've never read the Bible and I've only been in a church a few times in my life. Sometimes that's a major drawback when most of the people you know are going around quoting from the Bible and talking about creationism and being saved. It puts you at a real disadvantage. Maybe I should read the Bible so I can talk to more people. Also, it might help if Ellie and I ever write any more letters to the governors. We could drop in some quotes from the Bible that would make them feel very guilty. Things like *Thou shalt not kill.* I wonder where that is in the Bible.

"About Ben Cooper," Stephanie says. "I think he likes you."

I can feel my face getting hot, but I shrug and pretend not to notice. I'm sure I look like an idiot. Maybe I should transfer to another school where no one knows me. No wonder everyone says girls study more at all-girls' schools.

"So you like him, too," Stephanie says. She grins at me and we both start to laugh.

On Wednesday, when I get to world history class, everyone is talking about Coach Morrison. He resigned over the weekend. I've never heard of a teacher resigning in the middle of a school year. I don't think it's very mature behavior. I think Coach should have waited till after Christmas, at least.

That's what I tell Ben. He's wearing a green sweater today that exactly matches his eyes. I hope he doesn't notice that I have a new pimple on the left side of my face, just under my mouth. I turn around in my desk so he can just see my right side. I hope I haven't developed any new pimples since I looked in the mirror five minutes ago.

"Oh, God," Ben says. "Get real, Sarah. He didn't resign because he wanted to. He *had* to. The football team was oh-and-eight. Half the parents wanted to lynch him."

"Are you sure?" Mom doesn't care about football, so I haven't heard any complaints about the team. I knew it was doing pretty badly, though. "I thought this school really cared about education."

Ben rolls his eyes. "If the school really cared about education, do you think Coach Morrison would have been teaching world history?"

I turn around and listen to the substitute teacher. She's about a hundred years old, and she's very bent over, like she's looking for something on the floor. Her name is Mrs. Archer and she talks in a whisper. I wonder where all these substitute teachers come from. It's kind of like a horrible farm that keeps putting out bad crops.

Anyway, everyone ignores Mrs. Archer. Ashley Skiles spends the whole hour looking at herself in her makeup mirror and putting on mascara and blusher. It's very annoying. How can you concentrate on world history when someone like Ashley is putting on makeup? I hope she has to wear lots of makeup because she has so many pimples. Mom told me that when she was in high school, sometimes people would get really bad complexions. It's called acne, and she says no one seems to get acne at my school these days. That's too bad. I wish we could make an exception for Ashley and Emily.

All the way through the class, I think about Coach Morrison and what Ben said about him. Coach was a terrible teacher, if you want to know the truth. He'd been teaching world history for centuries, but he didn't know much about it. Also, he had a strange way of teaching. If he didn't like a civilization, he just ignored it. We skipped over two chapters about the Greeks last month. Coach said the Greeks were a bunch of losers, and he didn't think we could learn anything by studying about losers. Coach had already told us that we were going to be talking about American history the whole second semester. He said it was a lot more important than anything else in world history, except for Jesus Christ. He especially liked to teach about wars and how Americans never start wars, but they always win them. I heard that last year he spent two weeks on the war in Vietnam and how we could have won it if Lyndon Johnson had just had more guts. He said he thought that was because LBJ had grown up in Texas but he never played high school football. Playing high school football teaches you a lot about war, he said.

So I know that Coach was a pretty terrible teacher, but he was kind of a nice person. And he really loved this high school. He always talked about how it was the best public high school in the whole country and how he was so proud to be coaching here. He said he wanted that on his tombstone. I wonder how he feels about that now.

Also, I hope that Coach has enough money. I think

this is the way homeless people start out. They're doing fine and leading a normal life and driving a car and living in a pretty nice house, and then they get fired. I read a story in the newspaper last year about a homeless man who used to have a very good job at an advertising agency. But then he got drunk at an office party and mooned a big client and the next day he was fired. After that, he lost his family and his house and his car and he ended up panhandling at an intersection on Turtle Creek. The reporter tried to make the story sound kind of upbeat, though. It showed how the man used all his advertising skills to make a cardboard sign that made cars brake and give him more money than most panhandlers got. The sign said, *I Used to Be Exactly Like You.* Mr. Daniels, our journalism teacher, said that was a very good example of taking a different angle to a story.

I hope I don't see Coach out on Turtle Creek with a cardboard sign someday. It would be very depressing. I wonder if it would be better to pretend I don't see him or give him as much money as I can. It must be very embarrassing to get money from your former students. I wonder if all the parents who tried to get rid of Coach Morrison feel proud of themselves. I don't think I could fire someone in a million years, even if they were doing a terrible job. I hate to hurt people's feelings.

I walk out of class behind Ben and then he turns and touches me on the arm to say something. I feel like someone's splashed warm water all over me. I think I'm even more in love with Ben than I used to be. I feel like I'm floating.

Thursday night, I go downtown with Joe to watch Mom tape her show. He and I sit behind one of the cameras and watch Mom cut up a bunch of carrots and zucchini and squishy little tomatoes and pour them into some broth on the stove. Mom scrapes the vegetables off the cutting board and into the soup, and one of them falls in hard and splashes broth on her gold silk blouse.

Mom glances down at the stain and shrugs for the camera. "This is why a good cook should always wear an apron."

The two cameramen start laughing and so does Mom. She says, "Until next week, this is Dinah Morgan ... cooking up something Texas fresh ... and kitchen friendly." She smiles at the camera.

"Cut!" somebody yells.

Mom stops smiling and glares at the spot on her blouse. "Dammit to hell, this is a brand-new blouse."

Paul Stogner, the director of her show, comes up and starts talking to her. He's about as short as I am and he has scraggly brown hair that falls all over his

T-shirt. People who aren't in front of the camera can wear anything they want. Most of them try to dress as badly as they can. That's how you can tell the difference between them and the on-air talent. That's what they call the people on the air—*the talent.* The talent is always dressed in bright colors and wears about three inches of makeup and their faces are very perky, like they've just opened a present they really wanted.

Mom says that's the worst thing about being on TV. She hates to look perky. She says that someday she'd like to have a program called *The Depressed Cook,* and she'd wear a flannel nightgown and make all kinds of soft, lumpy, high-fat foods like mashed potatoes and macaroni and cheese and carrot cake with cream-cheese icing. People could watch the show when they were feeling bad, she says, and then they could stuff themselves with lots of carbohydrates. With a show title like *The Depressed Cook,* she says, she'd never even have to smile.

"I'm hungry," Mom says. She bends over and kisses Joe and then me on the cheek. "Let's get out of here."

Joe drives us to a Tex-Mex restaurant where you can smell the tortillas and refried beans the minute you get out of the car. Inside, there are Christmas lights draped across the walls, and they twinkle on and off. All the waiters are running around with trays over their heads, yelling at each other in Spanish.

Tonight I'm going to eat anything I want. Last night I weighed myself for the first time in weeks, and I've lost six pounds. I think it's because I'm in love. Stephanie says that once you start having sex, you get even skinnier because sex is such great exercise. That's very good news. Stephanie says her father wants to write a book about it called *Why Starve Yourself When You Can Feast on Sex Instead?* I'm not supposed to tell anyone about it, since Dr. Rider is afraid someone will steal his idea. He says that not many people realize that if you have sex for an hour, you'll burn off 675 calories. If you're really serious about losing weight, he says, you could have sex for two hours a day.

Ever since I heard about how sex was such great exercise, I've been going through the halls at school trying to figure out who has sex all the time and who doesn't. I guess all the really thin girls–like Ashley and Emily and Meredith Jennings–must be having sex constantly. Sometimes when I'm in the cafeteria line or putting my books in my locker, I hear rumors about sex, too. Guys like Alex Baxter brag about having sex, but you never hear girls talk about it the same way at all. One time I heard a girl in gym class tell someone else, "Well, I was drunk Saturday night. I don't know what I did." She raised her eyebrows and shrugged, and they both laughed. Stephanie's father says that happens a lot. Girls get drunk so they can have sex and then they feel like it isn't their fault.

I think that's stupid. What if you get very drunk the first time you have sex and you can't even remember what it was like or what you're supposed to do the next time? You might not even know if you enjoyed it. Or what if you didn't know if you were still a virgin or not? That would be a very big problem. Stephanie and I have promised each other that if either of us has sex before the other, she'll stay sober so she can describe every detail to the other person. That's fine with me. I don't like to drink, anyway. One time I tasted a glass of wine at Nana's house and I hated it.

Mom and Joe order margaritas and I get a Coke with a cherry in it. We all eat lots of chips and salsa. Mom tells us about how the ratings from her show have gone up, and the TV station wants her to think about writing a cookbook they can market with the show. After she finishes telling us that, she smiles at Joe and me and says, "You're my two favorite people in the world. I'm so glad we can have this much fun together."

Mom's never said anything like that before to me. I think it's just because she has to. Since I'm here, she can't say anything to Joe by himself. She has to include me. But she looks so happy that for a minute, I wonder.

Maybe she does love me, kind of, even if I'm not the daughter she wanted. That's what Dad always told me. He always said that Mom loved me even if I didn't realize it.

"Cheers," Mom says.

The three of us touch our glasses together. From the next room, I can hear the mariachis start to play.

10 ten

The next day, after my last-period class, I stop by my locker to pick up my algebra book. Ben's locker is a few feet from mine, and he's kneeling in front of it. He's tall and thin, and he has really rosy cheeks and dark green eyes. He has a small brown mole on the left side of his chin. If it were on a girl, you'd call it a beauty spot. I stare at it sometimes. I wonder what it would feel like to touch it, just lightly.

I can always tell when Ben's close around. I can almost feel him. I feel warmer inside and almost like liquid, like one of those soft, runny chocolates you get on Valentine's Day. It's very hard to act normal when I know Ben's there. I feel like my face turns pinker and my voice gets higher. I think it's strange, because Ben and I used to be friends when we were younger. He always made me laugh, and he still does. But now it's different. Ever since I fell in love with him, it's harder to be around him. I want to get farther away so I can start daydreaming about him again. That's too bad. Love is really hard on friendships, I think.

I watch him out of the corner of my eye. I've developed very good eyesight like that. It's called peripheral vision, and animals have it, too. I can see lots of things when I'm pretending to look straight ahead. Ben has on a soft, plaid shirt and blue jeans. His blue jeans have a crease down the front legs. I can see that really plainly, because the blue jeans have just stopped by me. Good Lord. What do I do now? What should I say? Maybe I should just stay here, crouched on the floor.

I slam my locker shut and stand up. I hope I don't faint or break out in lots of pimples or start twitching. I wonder how Emily Reif would act right now. Probably very cool. I'm not a cool person, though. I'm too nervous to be cool. Also, too much in love. I'll probably be ninety years old, living in a rest home, and I still won't be cool. I'll always be a big mess like this, and by then I'll need adult diapers, too. I bet Ben's already regretting that he stopped by my locker. Who could blame him?

"Hi," I say.

I haven't stood this close to Ben in a long time. He's gotten taller. My eyes are at the same level as the mole on his chin. If I got up on my tiptoes, I could kiss it. I'm sure he knows what I'm thinking. All I do is think about kissing him. He'd be completely disgusted if he knew. Maybe I should just pretend to pass out and he would call the paramedics and they can bring the ambulances and siren and take me out on a stretcher. It would be a lot less embarrassing than this. *High School Girl Overcome by Passion Is Treated and Released at Area Hospital. Educators Say This Is Another Sign That Today's Youth Have the Moral Standards of Chinchillas in Heat. "I was just walking by, and she threw herself at me," a clearly shaken, unidentified high school male said. "I was so embarrassed that I went home and vomited and read the Bible for three hours. You know the part about Sodom and Gomorrah?"*

"Hi," he says. His voice is wonderful, a little husky. I'll never forget how he said that. *Hi.*

All of a sudden, we're walking together through the hall. I'm pretty sure there are lots of other people around, because I can kind of see them, and lots of noise and people yelling and laughing and banging lockers. But all I'm aware of is Ben, walking along beside me. Close enough to touch. Just walking, except even walking feels different right now. It's more like gliding.

What does he want? Does he want to borrow my homework from world history? Does he really want to walk with me—or did he just almost trip over me and now he's stuck? Where does he want to go to college? What does he want to major in? Does he think the prison system works? What does he think about long engagements? How many children does he want? When did he get his braces off? Is his mouth as soft as it looks?

We've managed to walk about three miles through the school, and neither of us has said anything. I'm racking my brain to think of something to say that won't sound too moronic. *Great weather for November, huh?* That's the most original line I can think of, which is why I don't say anything. What do other people talk about? Aren't you supposed to ask boys about themselves? I think that's right. I read that somewhere, in one of those teen magazines where you see gorgeous, high-fashion models who tell how awful it was to be tall and skinny in high school and how they never had any dates, but now they're radiantly happy because they have a major cosmetics contract and a talk show and a great hairdresser and every time they enter a room, grown men swoon and propose to them.

Ask him about himself. But what? *Excuse me, but what do you think about the British monarchy?* That's not very personal, though. Besides, what if he thinks the queen should be beheaded, just like Marie Antoinette, and he doesn't know I'm against capital punishment? We'd get into a big argument and then we'd stop speaking to each other and that wouldn't be very good for our relationship, even if we don't have a relationship, exactly.

I feel like my mind's some kind of crazy popcorn machine. I hope Ben hasn't noticed that I'm very close to a psychotic breakdown, just like a woman I saw on a TV show. She had to be sedated for six months, then she escaped from the mental institution and got run over by a driver's-ed student. I think that's because people are very intolerant of mental illness and they just didn't want to bring her back on the show. I may write some letters about it after I finish my homework. Soap operas should be a lot more socially responsible.

I look at Ben out of the corner of my eye and he catches my glance and we both smile. He looks a little nervous, too.

He holds the door open for me, and we walk outside. It's finally gotten cooler, and the sky is a bright, beautiful blue. It's the most beautiful sky I've ever seen.

"See you," he says.

"Yeah." I pretend to be looking for my ride, but I'm really watching him while he walks off. I stand there, humming a tune I can't quite remember. It has love in the title, though, I know that. Out of the corner of my eye, I watch Ben get smaller and smaller, and I'm pretty sure I've never been happier in my life.

* * *

After I get home, Stephanie telephones to say that she's heard from Janice Monroe that Ben is going to call me up and ask me out that weekend. I have an article due for journalism class and an essay for English, but after her call, I can't do anything. I just sit and stare out my window. Every time I try to start working, my mind drifts off, and it feels so wonderful to think about Ben that I just can't stop it. I have no self-control at all.

The phone rings and I jump. I try to say hello using a low voice. I read that boys really like that. Stephanie says they think it's sexy.

"Sarah! Is that you?" It's Nana. "Your voice sounds very peculiar. Do you have a cold?"

I say no, I've just been studying very hard. Sometimes that makes my voice sound funny.

"Vitamin C is good for colds, Sarah. You should be drinking fresh-squeezed orange juice at least once an hour. You tell your mother that. She may think she's a cooking expert, but she doesn't know anything about vitamins."

I bet Ben is trying to call me right now while I'm on the phone with Nana. I wish we had call waiting, like every other family on earth. But we don't. Mom hates call waiting. So if Ben calls, he'll hear a busy signal and then he'll hang up. Or maybe he'll call someone else. I tell Nana I have an important test to study for and I need to go. That's what I always say. Nana probably thinks I work harder than any high school student in the history of the world.

"You know, I don't usually have time to watch your mother's show, Sarah. But my friend Esther saw it last week. She said Dinah looked puffy faced. Also, Esther tried to make the same dish your mother did. I think it was something very fancy, like your mother likes to cook. Pigeon in orange sauce or something like that, since plain food isn't good enough for her. Esther said it wasn't fit for dogs."

Great. Nana must be having a bad day. She usually slips in a few nasty remarks about Mom and then she hangs up. Today she sounds like she wants to talk. I can tell she's winding up and she'll be ready to talk for an hour about how horrible Mom is.

One time I asked Mom why she and Nana didn't get along well, and she said she'd rather talk about anyone in the world but her mother. So I asked Dad about it. He said that every time he watched a public television show about insects or reptiles that eat their young, he thought about Nana. Except Nana wasn't as attractive as most insects, he said.

That didn't help me at all. I still don't understand why Mom and Nana hate each other. Once Mom said she hoped she and I wouldn't have a terrible relationship, the way she and Nana did. She looked at me very closely when she said that.

"I have to go, Nana. I really do."

Nana sighs. "Well, I can see you have better things to do than talk to your grandmother, Sarah. Be sure you tell your mother what Esther said about her show. Dinah could use some constructive criticism."

I will, I say. Then I hang up and wait for hours for the phone to ring. When it finally does, it's Stephanie. She just had a conference call with two of her friends, and she found out Ben won't be calling me tonight. They all think he's going to call next week, though.

That night I spend the night at Stephanie's. Dr. and Mrs. Rider leave to go to a benefit for the homeless. I read about it in the newspaper today. The article said that as a very special treat, two homeless families were going to be invited to the banquet. That's what it said—a very special treat. I read the article twice so I could figure out who it was supposed to be a treat for, the homeless families or all the rich people who were going to the dinner. But the article never made it clear. That's what we've been studying in journalism—making articles clear. You're supposed to write so that someone with an eighth-grade education can understand what you say.

It's cool outside, so Stephanie turns on the gas fireplace with a remote control, and we sit in front of it. Stephanie unpacks her Ouija board. She has to hide it from her father, since Dr. Rider thinks that it has something to do with the occult and Satanism. But Mrs. Rider says it's okay. Stephanie's mother is always having her horoscope read and taking yoga classes, and that's not exactly Christian, either, Stephanie says.

"Oh, spirits!" Stephanie says. She's weaving back and forth over the Ouija board, like she's really dizzy. We both have our hands on the wedge, but I'm not weaving the way she is. "Oh, spirits! Tell us who likes Sarah! We need to know today! Tell us now!" Stephanie's eyes are screwed shut, but I'm watching everything that happens.

The wedge moves slowly and spells out *B-E-N*. When it finally stops on the *N*, Stephanie's eyes pop open. "My God," she says. "It must be true! The spirits never lie."

Maybe not, but I wish someone would tell Ben about the spirits. If he doesn't ask me for a date in the next six months, I may fall in love with someone else. When you're fourteen, you don't have a very long attention span, especially these days. I think it's because we've had TVs and VCRs and computers our whole lives. Sometimes I think that even though Ben talks to me a lot in world history class, he's almost as shy as I am. I don't see how anybody could be that shy, though. I think that girls have much tougher lives than boys. All boys have to do is play sports and it doesn't matter what they look like, really. Dad always said it was hard on boys, because they had to call up girls and ask them for dates and risk rejection. But I think that anything would be easier than trying to be pretty and thin and hanging around by the phone, waiting for it to ring and then picking it up and it's always somebody like Nana.

Mom says that being a girl is a lot better than it used to be, though. She gave me a long speech about how we can all have careers now and girls my age don't pretend like they're dumb around boys and we can do anything we want. She also said that girls were better off today, because at least they could be friends with each other instead of competitors. When parents tell you stuff like that, you realize they wouldn't know reality if it slapped them in the face. Mom wouldn't believe how nasty girls are to each other. Sometimes I'm nasty, too. I make fun of other people. I'm not nearly as nice as I used to be. I don't think anything has changed in the past century. I think it's all the same.

“I’m very hungry,” Stephanie says. “When you’re in contact with the spirits, it’s so much work that it depletes you. I need to eat brownies. They’ll build up my strength so I can do the Ouija board again. Maybe the next time we can contact a dead person to give us advice. Who’s the dead person you’d most like to talk to?”

She and I go into the kitchen and sit at the table. “We can only have five brownies apiece,” Stephanie says, putting the pan on the table. “I’m on a diet, kind of.” She cuts the brownies with wide sweeps of her knife. Then she turns on the radio. “You’ve got to hear this show, Sarah. Have you ever heard Dr. Lisa? My dad hates her. But I think she’s a riot. Listen to this.”

There’s a little static, then you can hear a voice. “You’re an idiot,” the woman on the radio is saying. She sounds like a speeded-up foghorn.

“That’s Dr. Lisa,” Stephanie hisses.

“You’re a total, complete idiot,” Dr. Lisa says. “If I were your wife, I’d beat your brains out for cheating on me. Your wife must be even dumber than you are—”

“Well, I—” a man’s voice begins.

“Don’t interrupt me,” Dr. Lisa says.

“Oh. Okay.”

“It’s hard to be a radio therapist. I hate to be interrupted—especially by idiots. So shut up while I’m thinking.”

"I'm sorry."

"I said to shut up, John. Apologies don't cut it with me. I'm not your wife, remember? I'm not the one you gave genital herpes to, am I?"

"No, but–"

"God–isn't Dr. Lisa wonderful?" Stephanie says. "Do you know what a dominatrix is? That's a woman who gets on top when she's having sex. I think Dr. Lisa is a dominatrix. That's what I want to be when I grow up. You have much better orgasms if you're a dominatrix."

She and I sit and listen to Dr. Lisa tell a bunch of people that they're so incompetent they should probably jump off a cliff and stop bothering her. We eat about a hundred brownies, too.

When Stephanie finally turns off the radio, I tell her about how Ellie and I used to watch *The Hallelujah Chorus* on TV. That was a televised revival they used to have on Saturday nights, and it had a preacher named Brother Bob Davis. Brother Bob had silver hair that looked like a spray-painted tumbleweed, and he wore dark glasses and skintight black pants. "I'm tryin' my best, my utmost best, to heal all you sinners in the Metroplex!" That's what Brother Bob always said. He'd scream it into the microphone. "Praise the Lord, I'm doin' the best I can! Praise the Lord!" Then Brother Bob would close his eyes and pray out loud. "Take me as I am, Lord. I'm just a poor sinner, like ever'body else. I can only do so much!"

About that time Brother Bob would start crying and a message would flash on the screen. YES! I WANT TO HELP BROTHER BOB CLEAN UP MY LIFE! CALL 1-800-BLESS ME.

Ellie and I used to call that number. One time Ellie called up and said she was Ashley Skiles. "I was so moved by Brother Bob that I just couldn't stand it," she said. "Hallelujah! Yes, I want to give ten thousand dollars. Praise the Lord! I'm going to take the Lord into my life instead of the whole football team. No, wait! Hold on! The Lord's speaking to me right now! He says I need to give twenty thousand dollars instead!"

By that time Ellie and I were rolling on the carpet, screeching with laughter. I hardly made it to the bathroom. One time I called Brother Bob and asked him if a religious experience felt like an orgasm. If it did, I said, I was going to convert and become a Christian immediately. Whoever answered the phone that time didn't have much of a sense of humor, because she hung up on me. If you're trying to convert someone to a religion, you should be more polite than that.

Ellie and I used to do things like that and we used to laugh all the time. We used to have a lot of fun together. But now I've hardly even talked to her in days, and I know she thinks I'm avoiding her. And I am. I know I am.

Thinking about Ellie, I feel terrible. I get a pain in my chest that squeezes my heart. What kind of person doesn't even speak to her best friend or go over to her house? That's not the kind of person I am, is it? I'm a better person than that. At least, I used to be. Maybe I'm not like that anymore.

I tell Stephanie those stories about Brother Bob and I try to make them as funny as they were when they happened, but I can't. The more I try to explain, the worse it sounds.

Stephanie looks at me and raises her eyebrows and shrugs. "I can't imagine Ellie Peterson doing anything funny," she says.

11 eleven

Stephanie says you have to be prepared for sex, since you never know when it's going to happen to you. For example, you could be out on a date with someone and, in an hour or two, you might fall madly in love with him. True love can come very quickly—just like that, Stephanie says. So it might be the perfect time to lose your virginity, but you have to be ready for it. You have to make sure you've shaved your legs and worn some really nice underwear. If you don't have really sexy underwear on, you might not have a good first sexual experience, Stephanie says.

That's why I ordered a Bazoom Bra. I wanted to be ready for sex. But also, I'm tired of being flat chested. Stephanie says all I need is a lift to get me started. After you start having sex and your body starts releasing more hormones, she says, your breasts grow like crazy.

Anyway, I saw an ad for Bazoom Bras in the back of a magazine. It was a very interesting ad. It said: *When You Wear the Bazoom Bra, You'll Raise More Than His*

Eyebrows! It had lots of little diagrams with arrows showing how your breasts get pushed up so high, they looked like guided missiles. A woman in a regular bra was in the *before* picture. She had dark hair that hung over her cheeks and she was looking down at her breasts, like it made her extremely depressed to see how flat chested she was. Then in the *after* picture, someone had given her a new hairstyle that bounced all over the place. Her hair was a lot blonder, too, and she looked very excited, kind of like someone had just pinched her or something. She had about three inches of cleavage in her Bazoom Bra, which was very hard to miss, since there were two red arrows pointing at it. Under her picture it said, "I used to hate low-cut sundresses. Now I love them! I can't wait to show off my new figure!"

There were more quotes from other women, and they all seemed to use lots of exclamation marks, too. J.T. from Little Rock said, "Ever since I got my new Bazoom Bra, my husband can't keep his eyes off me! (Or his hands, either!!)" B.B., age sixteen, from Las Vegas, said, "I used to be so unpopular, you wouldn't believe it. But now, thanks to my Bazoom Bra, my phone never stops ringing!"

I got excited when I read all those quotes. I wondered what I'd say when the Bazoom Bra representative called and asked for my testimonial. I wasn't sure I'd want my photograph in a magazine, though.

Today I finally got my new Bazoom Bra in the mail. Fortunately Mom isn't home yet, and I grab it and take it back to my room and unwrap it. There's a lot of tissue paper folded around it, with a card that says, *Every woman's treasure chest needs a Bazoom Bra!* The Bazoom Bra isn't very sexy looking. It looks kind of like a white dog harness. But I guess it needs *me* in it to be sexier. So I take off my old bra and put on my Bazoom Bra, and I can't tell any difference at all. Except it's very hard to breathe in the Bazoom Bra. I stare in the mirror, looking for my cleavage, and I finally see something dark, but it turns out to be a rib.

That's very disappointing. I can tell that if I wear the Bazoom Bra, it isn't going to change my life at all, except to make me pant a lot. So I take it off and wrap it up and write a letter to go with it and ask for my money back. Fortunately I'm very good at writing letters, since I've had so much practice writing all the governors of the states. I tell the Bazoom Bra people I feel defrauded. I like that word *defrauded* so much that I use it twice. Then I say I think that Bazoom Bra is engaged in fraudulent advertising and I'm planning to write an article about it for our school newspaper. That would make a very good investigative piece, but

I'd probably have to write about it anonymously. I don't want anyone to know how flat chested I am. Especially Ben.

I call Stephanie and tell her that the Bazoom Bra is a total failure. She says I should probably start concentrating on my legs and personality instead, and I should be very glad I don't have big breasts like hers, since they make it hard for you to have good posture. That's what people with big breasts always tell you. I don't believe it, though. I'd rather have bad posture and really big breasts. I've never heard about boys who ask you out because you have great posture.

I hang up and throw out all the testimonials from Bazoom Bra. If I put them at the bottom of my wastebasket and pile a lot of other stuff on top, I don't think Mom will even notice them.

The next day I go home with Ellie after school is out. She called the night before to ask me if I could. I didn't want to, but I said yes, anyway. Ellie sounded terrible over the phone. If I'd said no, she might have started crying. That would have been worse than going to her house. Sometimes you have to do things even though you don't want to do them.

It's the third week in November, and it's hot again. Some of the leaves have turned pretty colors, but it's about six hundred degrees outside. It's very hard to keep up with the seasons when the weather is so weird.

I think that may be why people around here decorate their houses so much, just so they can remind themselves what season it is. In the fall there are cornstalks and pumpkins outside most people's front doors, and in the spring there are Easter rabbits and big pastel-colored eggs. Everyone goes nuts around Christmas, too. Right after Thanksgiving, you can see truckloads of workmen putting up lights in people's yards and hanging them from the trees. It costs loads of money.

Last year Ellie and I thought about writing a letter to the newspaper about all the money people spend on Christmas lights, because Ellie thought it could probably feed all the starving people in the world for at least two months. But then the state of Texas executed three of the men on death row we'd written letters to the governor about, and we decided to have a candlelight vigil at Ellie's house instead. That was the time we both fell asleep with the candles still burning, and one of them caught an Oriental rug on fire for just a few seconds. Mrs. Peterson almost had a nervous breakdown about that. She told us the next time we held a candlelight vigil, we should have it at Ellie's father's house.

Around here, some of the mothers even decorate

themselves for the holidays. They wear things like jack-o'-lantern earrings and Santa Claus pins. They put seasonal collars on their dogs. Close to Christmas, you can see lots of minivans and Suburbans with wreaths and pine branches and red ribbons on them. It drives Mom crazy every time she sees one of those cars. She says that women in this neighborhood have way too much time and money on their hands, which is why they end up decorating everything in a fifty-mile radius.

Since I'm not religious, I get a little tired of all this religious holiday stuff. I think that's why we don't have any Jews in our neighborhood. When I was in the second grade, there was a girl in my class who was Jewish, and everyone used to watch her while we prayed to see if she closed her eyes. After that, she went to a private school, and some of the parents said that showed she wanted to be among her own kind.

This year, at the beginning of the semester, we even had a black kid who was a sophomore. He was the second black kid in the history of our school. His name was Allen and he was tall and very good looking. Everyone tried to be nice to him. Even kids like Alex Baxter who are revolting racists tried really hard to be nice to him. I think that was part of the problem. Every time Allen was around, people started acting too friendly and speaking in very loud voices, like

Allen was deaf or something. After a while, you could always tell that he was in a room because all the other kids were screaming and acting friendly. I think that's why Allen didn't stay. He left Hillside Park after the first six weeks and transferred to one of the Dallas magnet schools. I heard that he told everyone at the magnet school that he'd never seen so many blondes in his life till he came to Hillside Park. He couldn't tell them apart, he said.

I think about all these things because Ellie and I are walking along and we can hardly talk to each other. We seem to be too polite, the same way everyone was around Allen.

Ellie's lost weight, and she's very skinny. She seems almost like a shadow, because she walks with her hair hanging down over her face and stares down at the ground a lot. I've had better conversations with Nana. That makes me feel terrible. I know that it's mostly my fault, but I'm not sure what I can do. Sometimes I think I don't want to do anything—that I don't want to save my friendship with Ellie because she's so depressing to be around—and that makes me feel even worse. A good person wouldn't feel that way. A good person would stay with her best friend no matter what happened.

"You're friends with Stephanie Rider, aren't you?" Ellie says.

Her voice is very casual, but we both know she's asking an important question. If Stephanie and I are good friends now, that means Ellie and I aren't. I know that sounds stupid, but it's true. It's just the way things work in high school. Ellie and I were best friends and we spent all our time together, and we didn't have any other close friends. We always said that was because we were so liberal and socially conscious, and everyone else in school wasn't serious or smart enough for us. That wasn't true, exactly, but it made us feel better to say that.

But now I spend time with Stephanie and she and I laugh a lot, the way Ellie and I used to. And I know that Ellie and Stephanie wouldn't get along at all, so I don't even bother asking Ellie. Stephanie knows that I'm in love with Ben, and she's always getting her other friends to call him and ask if he likes me. She says her father told her that all boys and men either liked breasts or legs, and I need to find out which kind Ben is. If he likes breasts, then I should buy a new black-lace bra and hang around his locker and bend over a lot. Also, Ben could be kind of weird and get turned on by really strange stuff like good pedicures or girls who lick their lips all the time. After she told me that, I spent the whole day licking my lips every time I saw Ben. Then my lips got chapped, so I had to stop.

Sometimes Stephanie and I sneak into her father's study and read some of his books and look at all the good chapters about sex. I've learned a lot about sex since I started going to Stephanie's house. I know a lot about foreplay now, and I think I'd like to try it soon.

"'Lack of foreplay is one of the biggest complaints women have about their husbands,'" Stephanie read aloud from one of her father's books. It was called *The Eleventh Commandment: Bringing God into Your Bedroom for Greater Marital Bliss.* "'A considerate Christian husband will perform foreplay (see drawings one through thirteen for examples) for as long as it takes to arouse his wife. Even if it takes hours.'"

"Jesus!" She whistled. "Look at drawing one, Sarah! Maybe you should think about getting a considerate Christian boyfriend! Maybe I should, too!"

Every time Stephanie and I read one of those books, I keep wondering if Dr. Rider and his wife practice what he preaches. They only have two kids, so they probably had to use lots of birth control. Dr. Rider says that birth control is very important to a modern-day Christian marriage. He says that he respects the Pope as a person, but he thinks the Catholic Church is totally wrong about birth control. Dr. Rider says that he thinks God wants his children to use all kinds of birth control so they can have sex all the time and not have to worry about having babies. Look at Adam and

Eve, he says. They only had two children, didn't they? That was practically proof that there was birth control in the Bible. Dr. Rider says he wishes he could talk to the Pope about it. They could sit down and talk, just like two plain, ordinary Christians, even though the Pope is a Roman Catholic.

I guess what I like most about Stephanie, though, is that she doesn't make me feel sad all the time. I don't think there's anything wrong with falling in love or finding out about sex as long as you still get good grades. When we're together, Stephanie and I laugh so much that it makes me realize it's been months since I've had fun with Ellie. I'd just gotten used to her being that way.

When we get to Ellie's house, Mrs. Peterson is dressed up in a gorgeous tweed suit and high heels. Her hair's cut shorter and it's a lot blonder than it used to be. She's on the phone talking to someone. I can tell it's not Mr. Peterson, because she looks happy. That's what's really amazing about Mrs. Peterson. If you're not around her for two or three weeks, you hardly recognize her the next time you see her. It's very confusing.

Mrs. Peterson hangs up the phone and waves at me. "Sarah! Has Ellie told you? I'm studying for my real estate license!"

Ellie looks at me nervously. "No, Mom, I—"

"You haven't told Sarah?"

"No, well, not yet. I—"

Mrs. Peterson shrugs dramatically. "There's so much going on around here," she says to me. "There's almost too much to talk about. I feel so incredibly fortunate, Sarah, so very, very fortunate to have found a career I care about so much. And you know what else?"

Mrs. Peterson reaches out to touch my hand. She keeps staring right into my eyes. In fact, she's been staring at me the whole time I've been here. It's pretty uncomfortable.

"I've gone back to my maiden name," Mrs. Peterson says. "Linda Wagner. Doesn't that sound fabulous? That's been the key to the whole process. I feel as if I finally understand who I am."

She smiles at me, and I know I need to say something. But I can't think of anything, so I just smile and nod. It's hard for me to talk to Mrs. Peterson when she gets like this, because I know it never lasts more than a few weeks. Every time she does something like this, it's like she grabs everyone around her and makes them all go along and pretend that this time it's going to be different and everything's changed forever. I wish I hadn't seen her act like this again and again. I wish I could believe it was true. But I know it's not. I know she'll end up depressed and crying and staying in bed after this is over. I know that—and I know Ellie knows it, too.

"Our lives are wonderful right now," Mrs. Peterson says. She smiles at Ellie. "Wouldn't you say that, too, Ellie? Aren't we all happier than we've ever been?" Mrs. Peterson keeps smiling, but there's something hard about her face.

Ellie looks up through her hair. She tries to smile, but her lips are twitching a little. "Happier? Yes, we're happier...." Her voice trails off.

Mrs. Peterson puts her arm around Ellie's shoulder and squeezes it. Her nails are perfect red ovals on Ellie's white T-shirt. She pulls Ellie's hair back from her face and tucks it behind her ear. Ellie stands completely still. She stares down at the floor.

Mrs. Peterson smiles at me. She looks like a different person—happy and strong and excited.

When I was younger, I used to believe adults' faces and everything they said. But that seems like a long time ago. I look at Mrs. Peterson now and I see how desperate she is. I wish I could just see her face the way other people do. I wish I didn't know how hard she's trying and how sad her life is.

But I know it and Ellie knows it. Together we share too many sad things, I realize suddenly. Divorces and death and family problems and disappointments—and unrealistic dreams, like trying to save other people's lives.

Maybe that's it. Maybe that's why I feel like I have to get away from Ellie. That must be why I feel like I'm drowning every time I'm around her.

Mrs. Peterson takes Ellie, Madeleine, and me out for pizza that night. We go to a restaurant in a shopping center that has dim lights and about forty copies of the *Mona Lisa* on the wall. The minute we come in the door, Mrs. Peterson sees some people she knows and goes to their table to talk to them. Her voice is louder than it used to be and we can all hear what she's saying. Everyone in the restaurant can hear what she's saying. It's all about how she's studying for her real estate license and she's happier than she's ever been. It's very embarrassing. I hope no one thinks I'm related to her.

We stare at our menus till Mrs. Peterson gets back. She slides into her seat and pulls out her napkin. "Just mineral water," she tells the waiter. She must not think the waiter's rich enough to buy a house around here, because she doesn't give him a card. But he's very good looking and Mrs. Peterson smiles at him a lot.

Ellie and Madeleine and I share a large pizza that has long, stringy cheese and thick crust. Mrs. Peterson orders a salad and plays with it. Maybe that's a good thing, because no one else at the table wants to talk. Ellie's still looking down and Madeleine's eyes look kind of shifty and funny, so she may be taking drugs. Maybe she's sniffing glue. I wonder if her arm's healed. Nana called me yesterday and told me about a documentary she'd seen about teenage girls who mutilate their bodies with razors and scissors. It made me think of Madeleine and her arm. Could she have done that to herself?

"They're called cutters," Nana said. She always likes to know new terms like that. "They cut up their bodies and their parents never even notice. They're too busy with their own lives. Typical baby boomers, just like your mother. Do you like razor blades, Sarah?"

Sometimes when Nana says things like that, I realize that she must think I'm mentally retarded. I wonder what she did with herself before I was born. It takes up a lot of her time right now, thinking up different ways that I can die. I must be Nana's hobby.

"I've never seen such a quiet group in my life," Mrs. Peterson says. "Sarah—we haven't seen you in ages. What have you been doing?"

I say I've been studying a lot. That seems to satisfy Mrs. Peterson. Grown-ups always like to hear that you've been studying.

"The girls and I have been so busy," Mrs. Peterson says. "Did Ellie tell you we fired Margaret?"

I shake my head.

Mrs. Peterson shrugs. "I hated to do it, of course. It was sad. Margaret just hadn't grown enough. She couldn't keep up with us. I think she was threatened by my putting my life back together."

I'd seen Margaret only one time, about a year ago, at the Petersons'. She drove up in a black Volkswagen bug that had a bumper sticker that said *Visualize World Peace.* Margaret was there to drop off a present for Mrs. Peterson. She did that a lot. One time she gave Mrs. Peterson a towel that said *Women Are an Endangered Species.* She said that Mrs. Peterson should think about it every time she cleaned the kitchen and about how women were oppressed by the patriarchy. The trouble was, Mrs. Peterson never cleaned up anything. So the towel just hung in the kitchen for months.

The only time I saw her, Margaret was bringing a healing plant to Mrs. Peterson. I'd never heard of a healing plant before, but Ellie said they were very popular in Santa Fe. The plant was about six inches tall and it was very droopy. So was Margaret. She had circles under her eyes and she wore one of those bright, embroidered dresses from Mexico that didn't seem to match the rest of her. Even when she smiled, she looked like she was about to burst into tears.

"This should help," she said to Mrs. Peterson. It was one of those times when Mrs. Peterson was sleeping about fourteen hours a day and not getting dressed until the evening news was on. "Use this plant when you're doing your self-affirmations in the morning. It has a tremendous healing potential to it. Can you feel it in its leaves—the warmth?"

Mrs. Peterson touched the plant and said yes, she could definitely feel something. I wondered how Margaret could help her, since she looked so depressed herself. I bet Margaret was really upset when Mrs. Peterson fired her. Mrs. Peterson and Madeleine and Ellie had been going to see her for years, and I think they all went two or three times a week. They were probably half of her practice. I hope Margaret doesn't get to feeling worse and worse and drive her Volkswagen bug into a lake or something. For a therapist, she looked very suicidal to me.

"Do you miss Margaret?" I ask Ellie when we're back in her room. "I thought she was practically a member of your family."

Ellie shrugs. Her posture's a lot worse than it used to be. She looks like she's trying to be about a foot shorter than she is. "No, I think Mom was right about that." She shrugs again. Then she clears her throat. "I have a new list of people we need to write letters for. You wouldn't believe how long the list is. I think our society's getting crueler and crueler every day. It's very scary. I wish we could do more."

I know that if I ask Ellie why she looks so sad, she'd say it's because of all those prisoners on death row. But I don't think that's true. It's just easier for her to think about people she's never met and people who live far away. If she looked around at everything that's going on with Mrs. Peterson and Madeleine and Mr. Peterson and Misty and Blake, then she'd probably start sniffing glue or cutting her arms, just like Madeleine. The Petersons are a very screwy family. Maybe Margaret's lucky they fired her. Dr. Rider told Stephanie that you wouldn't believe how many completely crazy families live in our neighborhood. He says it makes him feel blessed to be a psychiatrist in a place like Hillside Park.

Ellie's expecting me to say something about the people on death row, but the truth is, I'm not that interested. I think you can be a good person in your own life by trying to not hurt people. Don't you? That's what I'm trying to do, and I hope it works. I don't think you have to go around writing a lot of letters and trying to save the lives of people you've never met to be a good person. I think there are lots of ways you can be a good person.

"I'm sorry," I say. "I just don't care about all of this as much as I used to."

Ellie's cheeks get redder and redder. "What do you mean, you don't care?"

What do I mean? I don't know. I mean all kinds of things. I mean I don't want to be the kind of person who spends weekends writing letters about total strangers that never save their lives—and maybe I don't want to save them, anyway. Maybe they've done something terrible and it doesn't matter if they get the death penalty. I mean that I'm here, spending the night at Ellie's house, but I don't want to be here. It makes me feel too sad and lonely to be here. I'm a different person now. I don't care about our friendship the way I used to. That's what I really mean, and Ellie and I both know it.

"I'm sorry," I say again. "I guess I'm just more interested in my own life right now than in anybody else's. I guess I've changed."

The room's so quiet that my words seem to echo over and over. The more times I hear them, the worse they sound. They make me sound like the kind of person who doesn't care about anyone else, but I don't think that's true. I like Ellie, but it's hard to be around her right now. I don't want to be her only friend.

I know I need to explain that better, though. So I try again.

"I want to be your friend. I know you're having a hard time." Ellie looks up at me and the color in her cheeks gets even darker. Her eyes look funny, too. They almost look like Ellie's angry. But Ellie never gets angry, except about social injustice. "Your family—I mean, having to live with your mother, and all the problems Madeleine's having. And your dad—the way he's all wrapped up in Misty and the baby ... and he doesn't ... well, it seems like he doesn't care that much about you and Madeleine—"

"You shut up!" Ellie's fists are clenched like she wants to hit me and her eyes are glittering. She looks like she hates me. "You shut your goddamn big mouth, Sarah. Don't you ever talk that way about my family again." She picks up a magazine from her bed and throws it across the room. "My family's fine."

I open my mouth and try to speak, but Ellie won't let me. "I told you to shut up," she says. Her voice is a high-pitched whisper. It sounds like she wants to scream, but she can't. "I'm sick of you criticizing my parents and talking about my family like we were all crazy. What kind of family do you think you come from, anyway? You always talk about your father like he was so wonderful. Well, he wasn't. He was a drunk and he practically died in the gutter. My father said you're lucky he didn't wipe out a whole family when he crashed his car. You're always talking about how perfect he was and how much he loved you. Well, he didn't. If your father loved you and your family, why did he drink so much? Why did he embezzle that money from your aunt's estate? Why did he—"

I put my hands over my ears and start to breathe really loudly so I can't hear what Ellie's saying. Then I pull a pillow over my head and sink back on the bed. If I close my ears, if I make as much noise as I can, if I cover my head with the pillow, then I can't see anything or hear anything. All I can hear is the noise I'm making and all I can see are the dark shapes of everything that used to be light.

Two days before Thanksgiving, Mom and Joe and I go shopping at the grocery store. We're in the frozen-food aisle when I hear familiar voices.

"Hello, Sarah!"

It's Misty and Mr. Peterson. Misty's wearing a bright yellow outfit that's so tight it looks like someone painted it on her. She's got on very high heels, too, that make her a little taller than Mr. Peterson. Mr. Peterson is carrying Blake on his shoulder. Blake is asleep, as usual. I don't think he has much personality, even for a baby. I've never seen him do anything but sleep. Also, his head is still kind of pointed. I think babies are supposed to grow out of that. He might look like that for the rest of his life.

Mom and Joe say hello. Mom has on that polite face she uses when she sees someone she doesn't like.

"It's so good to see you, Dinah!" Misty says. She comes up and kisses Mom on the cheek. That makes me sad. I'm always getting sad about stupid things like that. Ever since he married Misty, Mr. Peterson's been trying to coach her about being more upper class. That's why she's been doing more things like kissing people on the cheek and serving salads after the entrée and getting her hair fixed so it doesn't look like a big swirl of white cotton candy. I know I shouldn't feel sympathetic toward Misty, but I do. I don't think she's that bad. I think she's really in love with Mr. Peterson and now he's trying to change her so she's more acceptable and she can go to lawyers' conventions and country clubs and she won't embarrass him by saying something stupid. I wonder why he wanted to marry her so much if he was just going to change her. Sometimes, when the light is bad, I realize that Misty looks more and more like Mrs. Peterson, except she's a lot younger. I wonder what will happen to her when she starts looking older. I wonder if she ever thinks about that, too.

Mr. Peterson comes up and shakes Joe's hand, then he kisses Mom on the cheek, too. Mom doesn't like to be touched that much, especially when she doesn't like someone, and I can see her pull back. She'll be complaining about this for days, since she can't stand Mr. Peterson. She always says that if Misty had any sense, which she doubts, she'd string him up by his gold chains and let him twirl.

"You all heard about our latest family disaster?" Mr.

Peterson says. He doesn't wait for us to say no. "You remember Madeleine?"

We all nod. That's kind of a weird question, if you ask me. How could we have forgotten Madeleine?

Mr. Peterson shakes his head. "Kids. You give them everything and what do they do?"

No one says anything.

"They shoplift," he says. "Shoplift. I pay a load of child support, and this is what I get in return. Normal kids get picked up for Halloween vandalism. My kid gets picked up for shoplifting a parrot from a pet store and trying to set it free in the park. That's what happens when you have a mother like Linda, I guess." He pats Blake on the back and shakes his head some more. "If Madeleine wanted a parrot so much, she should have asked me for it. I've never denied my kids anything."

Mom raises her eyebrows and says, "Well, surely, if Madeleine returned the parrot—"

"Nah." Mr. Peterson starts to rub his neck. Then he runs his hand over his head. I think he's forgotten he doesn't have any hair. "Too late. Somebody's cat already took care of it. A twelve-hundred-and-fifty-dollar Central American meal, right down the hatch. Guess who's paying for it, too?"

Mom opens her mouth again, but she doesn't say

anything. She looks over Mr. Peterson's shoulder. That's what she always does when she doesn't like somebody. She can spend hours just looking over their shoulders.

I think Mr. Peterson's waiting for us to say something like how awful it is to have a daughter like Madeleine. But for a long minute, nobody says anything. I watch Mr. Peterson and try to figure out what his aura looks like. One time I read an article on auras and it said that they're made up of different colors, depending on what your mood is and what kind of personality you have. Even though I can't see it, I'm pretty sure Mr. Peterson must have a very dark aura.

"That's too bad," Joe says.

Mr. Peterson shrugs. "Didn't need to be paying out that kind of money. It's expensive, having a baby and a new wife, anyway."

There's another long silence. Then Misty starts talking. She tells Mom she has a great idea for a new TV show, and maybe they should have lunch sometime so they can discuss it. People are always saying things like that, and it drives Mom crazy. She says there's nothing more boring than someone with a great idea for a TV show, unless it's someone with a great idea for a book.

"I don't know if you remember," Misty says, "but I used to be a step-aerobics instructor. I'm retired now.

But there's really a very big demand for step-aerobics classes. I think it would make a great TV show. I've thought a lot about it. It's important for women to stay in shape, especially after they've had babies."

"Mmmmmm." Mom gives Misty a bright, insincere smile. "What a fascinating idea. We'll have to talk about it sometime, Misty."

Misty looks happy, like Mom's promised her a national show or something. She reaches out and touches Mom's arm. Then she frowns. "You know, you could use some toning on your upper body, Dinah. Your arms are a little flabby. I could help you if you'd like."

Mom's face freezes. She opens her mouth, but nothing comes out.

Joe puts his arm around Mom. Then he asks Misty how the baby's sleeping at night. He's very good about things like this. He's looking straight at Misty with an interested expression on his face, but he's rubbing Mom's shoulder at the same time.

Misty's face lights up and she starts talking about what a smart baby Blake is. She thinks he takes after his father and—

"We've got to go, Misty," Mr. Peterson says. He grabs her arm and pulls her away. Mr. Peterson usually gets bored if the conversation's not about him.

We all say good-bye and how nice it was to run into

each other. On the way home, Mom grumbles for about an hour about how Mr. Peterson is the biggest swine she's ever met in her life. When she thinks Joe and I aren't looking, she keeps running her hands over her upper arms.

"I haven't seen Ellie in a long time, Sarah," she says. "The two of you are still friends–aren't you?"

I feel sick just hearing Ellie's name. She and I haven't spoken since I spent the night at her house. When we see each other in the hall at school, we both look away. It's awful. But after what she said to me, I know I was right to stay away from her. She hated Dad, I guess. She must have been jealous because Dad loved me so much. She was just trying to make up something about him so I'd feel as bad as she does. There I was, trying to be nice to her, and she made up a big lie like that. Maybe she'd always been envious of me and trying to hold me back. She's a very pathetic person.

"We're not close the way we used to be," I say. "I think Ellie's a very unhappy person. I feel sorry for her."

Mom looks at me strangely and doesn't say anything. She's frowning and running her hands up and down her upper arms again. She must be really upset about what Misty said. I don't think anyone ever told

Misty you shouldn't insult someone if you were asking for a favor.

After we get home, I check the newspaper. There's a small article about Madeleine in it. *Fowl Play in Hillside Park,* the headline says. The article calls Madeleine a minor whose name is being withheld and it says she's been released to the custody of her parents. It doesn't say much more than that. But there's a picture right beside it. It shows the white grass at the park with a bunch of red and yellow and green feathers all over it. If you didn't know what happened, you'd almost think it was pretty.

Sometimes I think there are lots of ways people can leave you. Maybe you don't even know what's going on when it happens. It might take you years to finally understand it. I guess that it's gradual at first. It's so small, you don't even notice it. But when you're older and smarter, you look back and say, yeah, it started then. I didn't notice and I didn't understand it when I was living through it, but it was all starting then.

That makes me wonder. Is it better to understand things when they're happening or is it better to be happy? You hear people talking about things like a fool's paradise like it's something terrible. But maybe people who are stupid or foolish are the only ones who are happy. Maybe it's better to be like that. Maybe I should go back to being stupid and foolish. It doesn't hurt as much as being smart.

Right now, I'm having the best time I've ever had in my life. I have more friends and my grades are good and I'm even getting along better with Mom. Sometimes I think she might like me. But it feels like only a part of me—the outside part—is happy. All you have to do is touch me and I feel sore. I feel like every part of my body and my mind and my heart hurt. If I slow down, if I stop moving, then I feel terrible. That's why I keep moving. Lately, every day, I get up and jog. Mom's been nagging me to get more exercise for years. But now I'm finally doing it. It makes me feel better. I get up in the dark and I run and run till there's sweat pouring down my body. When I'm exhausted like that, when my body aches and my feet hurt, then I don't feel so bad. If I push myself and fling myself into things, then I don't feel so bad.

I only feel bad, really, when everything's quiet and I'm by myself. That's when I put my fingers in my ears and pull my pillow over my face, the way I did that night at Ellie's. I hate it when things like that happen. It's mostly late at night, when I can hear the grandfather clock in the living room. Every time I hear it, I realize I've gone another hour without sleeping. Sometimes when I can't sleep, I sneak into the liquor cabinet and pour myself a glass of bourbon. If I pour a big enough glass, then it helps me sleep. I don't drink it, though. I'm not a teenage alcoholic or anything. But I like the way it smells. It always makes me think of Dad. And it makes me happy, even though I know it shouldn't.

I've told you so much about Dad. I hope you can understand what he was like and why I loved him so much. I know I haven't told the whole truth, but you have to understand why. I didn't have that truth. I didn't want it. I couldn't have it. Carrying it around, I couldn't even walk. That's what it looks like in my mind. If I tried to carry it, I couldn't even move. I had to leave it there. I had to walk off without it. Does that make sense? I can't explain it, but that was the way I had to live.

I had a perfect life when Dad was alive. I really believed that, and I still want to believe it. But sometimes I can't. Sometimes I look back, and all the memories and pictures and feelings I have are changed. Someone's come in and moved them around, and everything's different. I don't know who it was. Maybe me. All I know is, I don't really know what's happened in my life. So much of what I thought I knew and what was important to me isn't true. I guess I should have figured that out a long time ago, but I didn't. Right now, I don't want to think about it. But sometimes I don't have any choice.

I keep thinking about what Ellie said that last time I was at her house. Even though I know she was trying to hurt me and she was lying about a lot of things, I can't stop thinking about what she said. About how Dad died drunk and how he could have killed somebody. Of course I know that's true. I knew that already.

Dad always drank too much. He always lived too big. He could do anything. He was good and kind and funny and smart—and so what if he had a few problems, like drinking? I knew that. I'd sneaked around listening to him and Mom argue. But he was still so big, everything he did was so big, that his faults didn't matter. They were part of who he was. We had to accept him as this wonderful gift—that's what I always felt. My father was this wonderful gift I'd been given. I never could believe my luck. He wasn't perfect. I knew that. But he was wonderful, fabulous, unbelievable, extraordinary. I could look those words up in *Roget's Thesaurus* and keep coming up with more and more adjectives. I could go on forever.

I know it's a strange way to feel about your father when you're my age. But Dad wasn't the usual father.

That's how I always felt. Till that night at Ellie's,

anyway. Something she said stopped me and I still haven't gotten over it. *If Dad had loved me, how could he have acted the way he did?* That was the one thing I understood perfectly in my life—that Dad loved me. It was unconditional love, like I told you. It didn't matter what I did or who I was or what I looked like. He thought I was wonderful.

I had that love, and I thought I still had it. But now, I keep hearing Ellie say that Dad must have not really loved me and part of me knows it's true. It's something that's been there, right in front of me, for a year, but I haven't wanted to look at it. I still don't. I don't want to go back. I want my past to be the way I've always thought it was.

But maybe Ellie was wrong about that. She was lying when she said Dad had taken money from Aunt Dottie's estate. Dad would never do anything like that, ever. He wasn't that kind of person. He wasn't dishonest. He was a good person. He'd never hurt anyone he loved, like Aunt Dottie.

If Ellie was wrong about that, then maybe she was wrong about everything. Dad loved me! She can't take that away from me. Dad loved me unconditionally, the way I always knew he had. Ellie was wrong. She is a sad, spiteful person. I shouldn't think about her anymore. I should try to forget everything she said to me.

* * *

As usual, Mom and I have Thanksgiving dinner at Nana's house. But this year Joe comes with us, too.

When we pick him up at his condominium, Joe's standing outside with a bouquet of fresh flowers. He has his hair slicked back over his head. When he sees me staring at him, he grins nervously. "It's not every day I meet someone like your grandmother," he says.

"Thank God for small blessings," Mom says.

Joe slips me some gum, and I pop it into my mouth. Mom and Nana both hate gum. But Joe says he always chews gum when he has a big case and he's feeling nervous. "I like two things about being a judge," he told me once. "It doesn't matter what I wear, since I put a robe over it. And I can chew gum anytime I want. That's what I call freedom."

He blows a big bubble and it bursts on his face. Mom almost drives off the side of the road. "Good Lord, Joe," she says crossly. "I'm a big enough wreck, anyway—going to Mother's house. I don't need bubble gum to push me over the edge."

"It's only for a few hours, Dinah," Joe says. "I'll try to keep the bubbles down." When Mom's not looking, he winks at me.

Nana lives in a big beige-brick house on Beverly,

which is supposed to be the swankiest street in Hillside Park. She has lots of faded Oriental rugs and oil paintings and gigantic antique furniture. The house and all the furniture make her look even smaller than she is. I think she's shrunk since the last time I saw her. She has a long face and jowls that hang on either side of her mouth. Today she's wearing a dress with a high neck and a cameo brooch. Like I said, Nana looks very sweet, like a harmless old lady, till you get to know her.

Next door a family has moved into a yellow Victorian house that's brand new. It has all kinds of towers and porches and railings. Nana says it's the most godawful architectural mess she's ever seen in her life, and she might not get her cataracts operated on if she has to look at big, trashy houses like that.

"This neighborhood is going to hell in a very ugly handbasket," she says. "The man's some kind of dentist. A dentist! Not even an orthodontist! How can a dentist afford a house like that? And the woman's name ends in an *i*. I can't even remember what it is. Sammi or Jessi or Debbi or something even worse. I can't stand names that end in an *i*."

I'm not sure how Nana knows how the woman's name is spelled, but this isn't a bad topic for her to be stuck on. At least she and Mom agree about architecture and first names they can't stand. This way, they won't have to start out fighting. They can wait till dinner.

Nana keeps on talking about how these people with new money are moving into the neighborhood and ruining it, since they're completely crass and have no taste or education or manners. Nana went to Vassar and she was in the class of 1949. She likes to bring that into the conversation as often as possible. She's still disappointed that Mom wouldn't even apply there.

"Now, you sit down, Dinah," Nana says. "I don't want you to lift a finger. You career women aren't any good in the kitchen."

Year after year, Nana says that. She's the worst cook on earth, since she likes to boil and bake everything till it turns gray-brown and you can't even tell what it is. But she never lets Mom go near her kitchen.

Nana picks up a bell and rings it. Nothing happens, so she rings it again, harder. You'd have to be totally deaf not to hear that bell, but no one comes, anyway. So Nana stands up and screams, "Josefina! Josefina!" For someone who likes to think of herself as being extremely refined, Nana screams a lot.

A maid, who must be Josefina, appears. She's dressed in a gray-and-white uniform, kind of like a pilgrim's outfit. Nana makes all her hired help wear uniforms. That may be one reason why they usually quit after a week or two. Then she usually accuses her maids of stealing the silver and makes them empty out their purses before they leave.

Josefina brings in platefuls of stale crackers and cheeses and puts them on the cocktail table. She looks pretty cheerful, so she must not have worked for Nana very long.

"This is my new maid, Josefina," Nana tells us. Josefina nods at us and smiles. "She doesn't speak English, so I'm trying to teach her. I see it as my Christian duty. Josefina's from Mexico, and she's got six children already. Six children at her age! It's a disgrace! I'm trying to teach her about birth control, too."

Wait till I tell Stephanie about this. I wonder what kind of birth control Nana's teaching Josefina about. Since Nana never, ever talks about sex or parts of the body, it must be hard. By the time she'd finished talking about rubbers or diaphragms, Josefina would probably think they were ornaments for the Christmas tree. I could see them hanging there, next to the icicles.

All the way through dinner Nana goes on talking about how life used to be so much better in the thirties and forties, when decent people lived in this country and everybody went to war together and doctors made house calls with small black bags and cured you better than all these big, flashy hospitals with all their bright lights and equipment and doctors who can't speak English any better than Josefina. She talks and talks and talks. Mom and Joe and I hardly have to say anything.

Nana gets so excited about everything she's saying that she forgets to make nasty remarks about Mom until we're about to leave. "Oh, I forgot to mention your television show, Dinah," she says. "What's the name of it? I never can seem to remember. I do hope it's going better, though."

Mom smiles, just a little. She looks at Nana out of the side of her eye. She never looks directly at Nana for some reason. Every time I see Mom around Nana, she acts different from the way she usually does. She's smaller and quieter, like she's not as alive or as tall as she usually is. It's funny to see your mother like that, especially when she always seems so strong.

"It's *Dining with Dinah*," she says. "And yes, it's going well, Mother. Thank you for asking."

Mom clears her throat and smiles. She's smiling the way she does on her TV show, when you know she's not happy but she's trying to act like she is, because that's what you have to do when you're in front of the camera. "We've had a lovely time, Mother. The dinner was wonderful. I'm afraid we need to go, though, so you'll have time to rest."

Nana tries to give us all her leftovers, and Mom says

that we have plenty of food—too much, as a matter of fact—in our refrigerator. But Nana doesn't listen. She rings her bell and screams at Josefina, who starts wrapping up dry slices of turkey. By now I'm pretty sure Josefina probably understands English better than Nana does.

"Well, I have enjoyed this tremendously myself," Nana says. "Seeing my only child and my only granddaughter—and you, too, John."

"Joe," Mom says. "His name is Joe."

"Joe," Nana says grandly. She holds her hand out to Joe, and for a minute I think she wants him to kiss it. Joe takes her hand and shakes it. He looks a little green, like he's on a boat that's making him seasick. I don't know if it's Nana or her cooking that's affecting him that way.

"You're so much better than Dinah's first husband, Joe," Nana says. "I always loathed him. I'm glad Dinah finally—after all those years—figured out how many problems he had."

"Enough," Mom says in a soft voice.

"His death," Nana continues, "was a blessing."

"Enough," Mom says again. Her voice is louder. "I won't have you talking this way, Mother. Especially not in front of Sarah."

This time she looks Nana directly in the eye and they stare at each other for one of those long minutes that seems to go on forever. It's terrible. I'm sure I can feel sweat rolling down my neck while nobody says anything. Finally Nana nods.

"I'm sure you think you know best, Dinah," she says. "I just wish I had more faith in your judgment."

"Fortunately," Mom says, "I don't give a good goddamn. After all these years, I don't give a flying fuck."

That's the last word anyone speaks before Mom and Joe and I head out the door. We don't even say goodbye to Nana, and Mom slams the front door shut like she was taking an ax to Martha Stewart. I'd always wondered if Mom knew the f-word, and now I have the answer. The only good thing is that now we don't have to take the leftovers with us.

thirteen

After we leave Nana's house, Mom and I drive Joe to his condominium and drop him off. On the way nobody says anything. We're all staring in different directions.

When we stop at his condo, Joe leans across the front seat and kisses Mom. "Are you all right, Dinah?"

Mom nods. He kisses her again. It's a nice kiss. I wish someone would kiss me like that. I wouldn't let him out of the car if he did, though. Probably by the time I ever get kissed, I'll be so sexually frustrated that I'll jump on him and won't let go. I don't think it's good to be that aggressive, but I might not be able to help myself. Stephanie says you can get lots of health problems like migraine headaches or warts or pimples when you're sexually frustrated. Maybe that's why I keep breaking out in pimples.

Joe gets out of the car and taps on the window and waves at me. "Happy Thanksgiving, Sarah."

As we drive away, Mom leans back and sighs.

"That's the last Thanksgiving we're ever spending with your grandmother," she says. "I know I should have stopped it a long time ago. It's not good for either of us."

The car slips through the streets. It's only late afternoon, but it's already dark. I don't like this time of year. It feels so gloomy and sad. Even when I'm feeling good, it makes me sad. I'm not feeling good right now, so it makes me feel terrible. I wish Mom would say something. I know she's feeling bad right now, but so am I. I wish she could make me feel better. But she's never been good at that. Even when she tries to talk to me, lots of times I just feel worse. I think we're out of sync. That must be it. We're so different that even when we want to be close, we can't be. It's almost impossible.

The house is cold when we get home. Mom turns up the thermostat and we both stand there in our coats and rub our hands together. "Let's make hot chocolate," Mom says.

We go in the kitchen and take off our coats. Mom puts some chocolate in the top of a double boiler. Then she adds some boiling water and turns on the heat till it foams. She heats it till it foams three more times. That's what you have to do if you want to have great hot chocolate, Mom always says. You have to take your time. You can't hurry too much. She and I stand in front of the stove and she stirs in hot milk and sugar. We don't look at each other. We stare at the hot chocolate while she stirs it again and again.

"Do you like Joe?" Mom asks.

I look at her face out of the corner of my eye. I think of how Joe lopes around like a big grasshopper, and how friendly and happy and kind he is. When he's around Mom, you can tell he thinks he's the luckiest man in the world.

"I like him a lot," I say. I can feel something else pushing its way up. Something I need to say. "But he's not Dad. I miss Dad."

"I know you do," Mom says.

All of a sudden, I don't care about what I'm supposed to say and what I'm not supposed to say. I'm tired of not saying things that I want to say, ever, and being polite all the time.

"Why did you and Dad get divorced? No one would ever tell me."

Mom stops stirring the chocolate and studies her hands. Ever since she and Dad got divorced, she hasn't worn a ring on her left hand. At first it looked like something was missing. Now it looks like it's always been that way.

"What could we tell you, Sarah? It was hard to talk about."

Mom stirs the chocolate some more, then she pours

it into two big mugs. She and I sit down at the kitchen table. We still don't look at each other.

Mom sighs. "We couldn't keep on going the way we were going."

"That doesn't tell me anything," I say. "What do you mean?"

Mom's quiet for a few seconds, and then she starts to talk. "I was married to your father for fifteen years. Even after all that time, he was still the most exciting man I've ever known. He was funny and he was smart and he was—he was more alive than other people. You know all of that."

I nod. Of course I know all of that.

"But I couldn't live with him anymore. He exhausted me. He drank too much. He spent too much money. It was as if—as if... I don't know... he took up too much space. I got to the point where I couldn't breathe around him. He was—what? I don't know how to say it—too oversized for me. He took up all the air in the room. There wasn't anything left for me. I felt crushed by him."

She turns and looks at me, and for the first time in my life I feel like she's asking me for something. "I know how much you loved him," she says. "I hated to hurt you. But I had to get out of the marriage. Your father wasn't going to change, ever. I couldn't ask him to change. How could I? But I got tired of being the only adult in the house."

I swirl my hot chocolate around in the mug again and again. Mom's never talked to me like this before. But in a way, she's telling me things that I already know. Maybe I didn't realize that I knew them, but they're familiar to me. Maybe I felt them even when I didn't recognize them. I hate what she's telling me, but I know she's telling me the truth.

"I don't blame you," I say. "I knew there were lots of things that were wrong."

Mom throws her head back and stares up at the ceiling. "I know Joe isn't your father. He's not at all like him. But maybe that's what I need.

"With your father, I was the one who loved him—the one who would have done anything for him. With Joe, it's different. He's the one who loves me. It's nice to be the one who's loved, for a change."

She and I sit there for a few seconds without speaking. Finally I ask Mom something I've always wondered about. Why hadn't any of Dad's family come to his memorial service?

Mom sighs. "They were bitter about what he'd done," she says softly.

"Because he had money and they didn't? But Dad never—"

"Oh, Sarah," Mom says. "Oh, baby. Because he embezzled money from Aunt Dottie's estate."

I can't sleep that night. I lie in bed and think about Dad. I recall those last weeks before his death.

I knew he was changing then. I didn't need Mom or any other grown-up to tell me. I knew he was out of control and getting worse. He was driving faster and drinking more. One night when he and I went to dinner, he got so drunk that he couldn't even drive us home. We had to take a taxi. I'd seen him drink for years, but it had never affected him like this. Dad had always been one of those people who could drink a football team under the table and then get up the next morning and play three sets of tennis and beat anybody on the court. He never exercised or took care of himself, but he was always fine after he had a little sleep. One time I heard someone say he was one of the best natural athletes he'd ever seen. I remember how happy that made me to hear that about my father.

Everywhere Dad went, people noticed him and talked about him. It was good, wasn't it? All that excitement, I mean. I remember the stories he'd tell about being so drunk he couldn't stand up, and how he talked his way out of a traffic ticket. Or how he gambled all his money on an oil well, and it came in—and he was even richer than he used to be. These were wild, wonderful stories, and they were true. They were the way Dad lived. If I loved Dad, I had to love his stories, didn't I? I had to love everything about him.

A few days before he died, he fell asleep at the wheel and rammed his car into a telephone pole. It was a brand-new red Cadillac, and he totaled it. But he walked away from the wreck. He made it into another funny story that he told. By then he had another new Cadillac, and that was the car he died in.

I still don't know what happened that night. I know he was with a few other people, but I never found out who they were. I guess he looked fine leaving the restaurant, but that's a stupid thing to say. Dad always looked fine. He could always handle his liquor. He laughed at people who couldn't.

He was on his way home when his car ran off the road and struck a median. They found him there, with the radio still playing and the headlights still on. He died from a massive heart attack—that's what the autopsy said. He never suffered. He never knew what happened to him. He was just there one minute, and the next he was gone.

I thought about that every day. I cried every day. I felt terrible because I wasn't even aware of that time, that instant, when Dad was gone. We'd always been so close, and I'd thought I would feel it when something happened to him. But I didn't. I was at home, in bed, asleep. I didn't hear about anything till the next day. I didn't even have a feeling that anything was wrong. I never suspected anything, till the phone rang and Mom's face went white. Even when Mom told me, it didn't make sense to me. People like Dad don't die. They're too big and vital. How can the world go on without them? I didn't think it could.

Dad was cremated, and we had a memorial service at a Methodist church, even though he wasn't a member of it. Lots of his friends got up and spoke about him. They told funny stories about him, and everybody laughed. They were stories I'd heard millions of times before, but I loved hearing them again. It was like having Dad there with me, to hear those stories again.

But then it was all over and we went home. I knew I was supposed to start living my life again, but I didn't know how to do it. Then everything started getting worse.

We found out Dad was broke when he died. That was surprising, because he'd been rich for so long. But he always said you had to be willing to go broke if you were in the oil business. It was almost a point of pride. If you hadn't gone bankrupt at least once, you weren't a real oilman. On the other hand, you weren't supposed to die broke. You were supposed to take care of things better than that.

I knew there was money missing. I knew that some of Dad's business partners were upset with him. Sometimes I could hear Mom on the phone, talking to them. "You know how Tommy was"—that's what I heard her say over and over. And they did. We all did. We all knew how Dad was.

There weren't any lawsuits and I guess there wasn't any evidence that Dad had done anything wrong. I knew some people were upset with Dad, but nothing was ever proved. I knew he'd been the trustee for Aunt Dottie's estate ever since she went into the retirement home. But I never knew he'd taken money he shouldn't have.

I knew that Dad cut corners sometimes. He was kind of sloppy like that. But he had a good heart—and that was what counted, didn't it? It was like his speeding when he drove. I can remember the first time I ever asked him about that. We were driving through West Texas, and Dad was going 105. I asked him what the speed limit was, and he said 75. "But that don't apply to us, darlin'," he said, and winked and grinned.

He meant to speed. He meant to break the rules. He never meant to hurt anyone, though.

But he did hurt people. He hurt me and Mom and

some of his business partners and Aunt Dottie and her family. It didn't matter what he intended. He'd hurt us all. He was the most generous person in the world, but he didn't act that way. He loved me more than anyone in the world will ever love me–I know that–but he left me alone.

How do I put that all together and make any kind of picture, any kind of story, out of it? It isn't working. It's too complicated for me. I can't do it.

It was so funny to me. I didn't quite get it for a long time. Dad had always been so strong and powerful. He could always take care of everything. But he died broke and alone. He lived big and he died small. Is that what happened?

I don't know. It doesn't make any sense to me. The more I know, I realize I don't understand anything. I loved Dad with all my heart, but I didn't know him at all.

Mom and I spend the rest of the weekend bumping into each other. We don't talk much. I guess we've said everything we need to say. We don't even watch TV together.

Nana calls me three times on Sunday. The first time she complains about the president. "He's a typical baby boomer, Sarah. Selfish. Spoiled. Promiscuous. Have I ever told you about those demonstrations they used to have when they were college students? It was disgusting. They were filthy and bedraggled.

"I feel sorry for your generation—being reared by baby boomers. They have no moral standards at all, Sarah. None. We pray for their souls every week in my Sunday school class."

The next time she calls, she tells me about a high school student in California who got run over by a truck after his car ran out of gas on a freeway. "An eighteen-wheeler, Sarah. The news says the truck driver was an illegal alien. Didn't I tell you those people were dangerous?"

Finally, when Nana calls me the third time, she asks if Mom is mad at her. "Dinah hasn't even called to thank me for Thanksgiving dinner—and I worked so hard on it. I brought her up to have better manners than that. Is there something wrong with her? Did she get offended about something?"

Nana's very good at asking questions like that and sounding very innocent. I'm pretty sure that she could walk up and stick a knife in you and then ask why you're so upset.

Dad used to tell me that I was good at understanding the way other people felt. Sometimes I think I'm almost too good at it. I listen to Nana's voice and I can almost see her face while she talks into the phone—how puzzled she looks. She never remembers what she's done, I know that. Or if she does, she's changed it so much that it looks completely different. If you were there, you wouldn't even recognize the scene you'd lived through. She sees the world with big chunks missing or replaced with something else. Do we all do that?

"I'm very concerned about your mother's behavior, Sarah. Do you think she's mentally unstable?"

Nana talks on and I listen to her voice. She tells me how she's always tried so hard to make my mother happy, and how nothing she's ever done has been good enough. She starts to cry. I know I'm supposed to say something now, about how Mom really loves her and didn't mean to hurt her. That's what I usually do. I try to make everything all right. I try to see Nana's point of view.

But today I don't feel like doing that. Even if Nana doesn't remember what she said, I do. Maybe I have to stop feeling sympathetic toward her. Maybe I just need to remember what I heard and what I saw at Thanksgiving. If I don't do that, then I'll never understand anything. I'll just go on believing what everybody tells me is true. I'll never figure anything out for myself.

"I see your mother has already talked to you," Nana says. "She's already convinced you of her story."

Her story. Nana's story. My story. Dad's story. Ellie's

and Mrs. Peterson's and Madeleine's and Mr. Peterson's and Misty's. I'm tired of all their stories. Why isn't there just one story that's the truth? Why can't it be easier than this?

"You said terrible things to Mom, Nana. That's what she's angry about."

Nana gasps on the other end of the line. Then she hangs up on me.

I'm standing there, right by the phone, when it rings again. This time it's Ben. He's calling to ask me out for next Saturday.

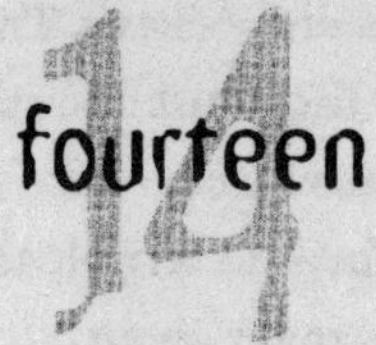

fourteen

Monday, after school is out, I go home with Stephanie. Mrs. Rider picks us up in her Jaguar, and Stephanie and I sit in the backseat so we can talk. I called her last night to tell her that Ben had asked me out, but she was at a Christian Promise group that her Sunday school sponsored.

Stephanie said the retreat, which was called *Promise the Lord!*, was the worst experience of her life. All the kids were jumping up and down, promising God that they wouldn't have sex till they got married. She said she'd spent most of her time trying to figure out if she was the only virgin in the whole room. "Ashley Skiles was there—I mean it!—Ashley Skiles. Ashley's slept with the whole football team, I'm pretty sure. I don't even think it was one at a time, either.

"And the girls—and I'm not kidding about this, Sarah—the girls get promise rings to remind them not to have sex," Stephanie says. "My God, it was awful. The rings were very tacky looking, and then everybody had to stand in a circle and sing a song about remaining chaste. They had to rhyme it with haste, of course. *Don't be in haste ... remain chaste.* I almost barfed. If they ever found out that my father was a Christian sex therapist, they'd probably stone me or something. They do that a lot in the Bible. That's why I don't read it anymore. It's too gory."

Stephanie throws her head back. "But that's not important. We've got to talk about you. What are you going to wear Saturday night? We have to get you ready. You think I should ask my dad what turns men on?"

Mrs. Rider keeps on driving and doesn't say anything. I'm kind of amazed every time I'm around the Riders. They all go around talking about sex all the time in front of each other. Stephanie says they also wander around in the nude, because her parents think the human body is beautiful and there's nothing to be ashamed of. I can't imagine walking around in the nude. Every time I spend the night at Stephanie's, I worry about that. What if I get up in the middle of the night and see her parents naked? I don't think nudity is a good idea when you're as old as they are.

Fortunately Stephanie has already timed them having sex. She says they have sex twice a week and it lasts about twenty minutes each time. When her parents make lots of noise, they always look happier the next morning, she says. They pat each other on the rear end when they're making breakfast.

"It's hard to concentrate on breakfast when they're doing things like that," Stephanie says. "I know sex is normal and healthy and everything, but I'd still rather not think about my parents doing it."

Maybe it sounds kind of weird that Stephanie's family goes around talking about sex all the time and Stephanie is still a virgin, even though she's already had four different boyfriends. She says that all her boyfriends were nice, sort of, but she knew she didn't want to lose her virginity with any of them. "I liked them, but I didn't love them," she says. "I think it's really important to be in love for your first sexual experience. The way you are with Ben."

But I think it makes sense, kind of. When your parents are really open about sex and they're practically dying for you to have sex so they can show how open-minded they are, the last thing on earth you want to do is have sex so you'll make them happy.

"They're a little too open, if you know what I mean," Stephanie says. "It's kind of like Madalyn Murray O'Hair's son becoming a born-again Christian. Have you heard about that? Maybe I'll become a nun. Did you hear that, Mom? A nun."

Mrs. Rider said yes, she had heard it, and she and Stephanie's father would support her in any decisions she made about her lifestyle.

"It's a joke, Mom," Stephanie says. "A joke. I'm not even religious—so how can I become a nun?"

At the Riders' house, Stephanie and I eat more Girl Scout cookies and watch TV and talk about school. We both have science projects due in January. I've always hated science projects, but Stephanie says I need to look at them more creatively. This year she's going to do her project on menstrual cycles and how they're affected by midterm exams.

"It's guaranteed to give Mr. Simon a heart attack," she says, crunching on a cookie. "I can hardly wait to tell him about it. I just love shocking people. I've already got my color scheme planned for the display and everything. It's going to be white with red splashes. I might paste a Kotex on it, too. How do you think that would look? I bet everybody would notice it, don't you?"

Sometimes I think Stephanie's a little way-out for me. I'm trying to imagine what it would look like to have a science project on menstrual periods in the middle of all those other projects about recycling and solar power and lasers. I hope Stephanie's talking about a new Kotex and not anything used. I'm almost scared to ask.

Sometimes being around Stephanie makes me think of Ellie. Stephanie's a lot of fun, but she likes to talk all the time. The truth is, she doesn't like to listen that much—unless we're gossiping or talking about sex.

I miss Ellie's quietness and the way she always listened to me. I miss her and I feel guilty about her. But it's too late. Even if we apologized to each other, we couldn't be friends the way we were before. *Things happen between people—and you can't change everything you want to. You can't always go back, no matter how much you want to.* That's what Mom told me one time. I think we'd just seen a movie and we were talking about it. But we weren't, really. When Mom said that, I knew she was talking about her marriage to Dad.

"My science project is part of the feminization of science," Stephanie says. "It's very important culturally. Dad says that if I have any problems with it, he'll be happy to lobby the school board. He says the American Civil Liberties Union would be interested, too."

She presses the remote control and switches from station to station. There are three ex-convicts on one of the talk shows. Under their faces it says, *Sentenced to Death—and Later Found Innocent.*

"My God, how depressing," Stephanie says. "They could have fried." She switches the station again.

"Ellie Peterson and I used to write the state governors about inmates on death row," I say. "We'd ask for them to be spared."

Stephanie looks at me in a strange way. "That's great. Did you ever save anybody?"

"No," I say. "Not that we ever knew."

When I get home, I have a message from Ben on my voice mail. I listen to it five times and then I save it in case I need to listen to it again. Ben has a very sexy voice. "Sarah—will you give me a call?" The way he says my name, I like it a lot more than I usually do. Maybe it isn't so bad after all. Maybe I won't have to change it to something more glamorous like Yvonne or Danielle or Layla after all.

I already know Ben's number by heart, since I've looked it up in the school directory about a thousand times. But I look it up again just to make sure. I just like to stare at his name. *Ben Cooper.* It makes me feel dizzy, just looking at it. I hope I don't have a fainting spell on our date. On the other hand, that would be pretty romantic if I fainted and Ben had to carry me somewhere. I let my head fall back and try to imagine what it would be like to be in Ben's arms. I'd hate to be unconscious and miss it. But what if I'm too heavy for him? What if I faint and he can't pick me up because I weigh too much? That's not very romantic. Maybe I'd better not faint.

I dial Ben's number, and while the phone rings I think of all the other stuff I know about him. His birthday is January 23. His father's a lawyer and his mother's a pediatrician. He has a younger sister named Becca. He has a dog and two cats, and he lives in a big, two-story house on Colgate with red brick and white trim. His family has a Jeep and a Lexus sedan without any bumper stickers on them. It's a good thing I took journalism this year. I'm much better at snooping than I used to be. Maybe if I start to date and my self-esteem improves a lot, I might still become an investigative journalist.

A girl answers the phone and I ask to speak to Ben. "It's a girl, Benjamin!" she screams. "Did you hear that—a girl! Oh, my God, you'd better hurry before she hangs up!"

"Shut up," I hear Ben hiss. "Hello?"

"Hi. It's Sarah."

After that, he and I talk for thirty-seven minutes. That's a long time. I wonder if that means he really likes me. Maybe he's just bored and doesn't have anything better to do. Maybe he feels sorry for me since I'm completely in love with him and he knows that I do things like lie around on my bed and look up at the ceiling and practice kissing him and talking to him in my head. Maybe he knows what a total drip I am.

"We still on for Saturday night?" he asks.

A nuclear war could start the night before and, as far as I'm concerned, we'd still be on. A tornado could level Dallas. An epidemic of smallpox could break out. A meteor could smash into the earth. I think of every disaster I can. I can't think of any that would be big enough to make me cancel the date. Well, maybe if I develop a lot of crusty pimples with pus oozing out in the next few days.

"Sure," I say. I make it sound very casual, like I've almost forgotten we have a date Saturday night and I've already made big plans to watch TV and pluck my eyebrows and floss my teeth.

"See you," he says.

I hang up the phone very carefully. A few minutes later Mom sticks her head in the door. "Dinner's ready," she says. She looks at me and frowns slightly and cocks her head. "You've got a funny grin on your face, Sarah. Is there anything going on I should know about?"

For just a minute, I wish she were the kind of mother I could talk to. It would be fun if she would throw herself down on one of the pillows in my room and talk about boys and dates and love. We could be the way mothers and daughters are supposed to be.

But we'll never be like that. Mom's just not that interested in me and my life, even though she keeps pretending to be.

"I've got a date Saturday night. With Ben Cooper. I think we're going to a movie."

"Ben Cooper? Who is he? Do you like him?"

"Just a guy in my world history class." I shrug. "He's all right."

Tonight on the news, there's a story about a woman who's on death row in Texas and she's going to be executed in two days. Ellie and I wrote letters to the governor about her last year, because we'd read about how she'd found God and was trying to be a better person, even though she did kill three people with an ice pick when she was a teenager. We wrote the letter together and I still remember it, because it was different from the rest of our letters. I guess it was because it was about a woman and maybe that affected us more. That sounds sexist, but it's true.

Anyway, we wrote how everyone can make terrible mistakes, but what good does it do for them to have to pay with their lives? We said we thought that this woman, Bonnie Shepherd, could do so much more with her life by helping other people not to make the same mistakes she had. What good does it do to learn something if you have to die right away? I thought that was a very good point.

I watch the news and see the photographs and video footage of Bonnie Shepherd. She's in her thirties now and her face looks thinner. But her eyes are still the same bright brown I remember, almost like something's burning inside them. I've never seen anybody who had eyes that color before.

I wonder how the governor feels when he sees her on TV. I wonder how it feels to be the person who takes her in the room and straps her to a table. I wonder what it's like to watch someone die. I wonder about all these things, but I don't feel like I care the way I used to. It all seems so distant to me. I don't want to be like that. I want to care about other people, the way I always have. I bet Ellie's watching the program right now, crying. But I'm not. I'm just watching it and my eyes are dry. Maybe I can't care about people the way I used to. Maybe I care too much about myself and my own life.

This week I realized I don't want to think about Dad any longer. Since he died, I've thought about him and thought about him—and now I'm ready to stop. Thinking about him hasn't done me any good, and I want to quit. I feel like here's this image I had of Dad—of his strength and energy and love and goodness—

and somehow it got smashed and I can't put it back together. Every time I've heard something new about him, I realize he's not the same person I thought he was. I feel like I lived my whole life listening to him lie to me and believing every one of those lies. Dad was more important to me than anyone else on earth, and I thought I was that important to him, too. That was one of those stories about my life that I believed, and now I don't believe them any longer and I don't know what's left. It's hard to know how to live when I can't even figure out what my life is.

Sometimes I look back and I feel like I hate Dad. Why didn't he care about me the way he always said he did? Why didn't he take care of me? Why did he lie to me over and over? Didn't he know I would have loved him no matter what? It was like I had to get used to his death, but then he died in another different way, too. He died fast the first time, and it was a shock. But this second death has been piece by piece, like he's been dying by inches—and I have, too. And every time I hear something new, it breaks my heart a little bit more. No, it's not like breaking. It's like shattering.

It reminds me of the time one of Nana's maids broke a vase in her living room. Nana kept saying what an expensive antique vase it was—and she pronounced it *vahhs* so it would sound even more expensive. Nana was yelling and the maid was crying, but for some reason I didn't pay that much attention to them. I was looking at the hardwood floor, where the vase had smashed. The pieces were everywhere—tiny and bright and jagged. There are so many pieces lying there, all of them separate. I looked at them and I couldn't believe they'd ever come together to make something that was whole.

fifteen

Ben picks me up at seven on Saturday. Well, if you want to get technical, it's actually Ben and his father. But I'm not a very technical person.

I hear the doorbell ring. Ben's exactly on time. That's good, I think. I can hear Joe and Mom answer the door. It's easy to hear because I'm standing just around the corner of the upstairs hall, peering down. I hope no one sees me. I look mentally disturbed, sneaking around like this, but I can't help it.

I've been ready for about three hours. I gave myself a manicure with a bunch of silver nail polish and I'm wearing mascara and some eye shadow and a little bit of lipstick. I hope the lipstick isn't on my front teeth. I've also changed clothes seven times. Right now, I'm wearing a red cashmere sweater with some black wool slacks. I don't want to get too dressed up. Stephanie says that shows you're trying too hard.

"Sarah—Ben's here!" Mom sounds pretty casual, like it's a normal thing for a boy to be picking me up and not like it's the first time in my life I've ever been out on a date.

I peer around the corner again. Fortunately they're not in the entry hall any longer. I think they've gone into the living room. I know it's supposed to be wonderful to make a grand entrance coming down the stairs when you're going out on a date. But I don't think I'm exactly the grand-entrance type. I'm pretty sure I'd catch my heel on the carpet on the stairs and turn a flip in midair and slide right down the stairs, with my nose bleeding all over the rug or something. I don't think that's the image I want for my first date. If that happens, I'll probably have to move to a Third World country and devote my life to working for the poor. It's too bad Mother Teresa is dead.

Mom and Joe and Ben are standing in front of the fireplace, talking. Actually, Mom's talking and Joe's laughing. Ben's not saying much. It's funny to see him like this. He looks nervous, and he's shifting from one leg to the other. He has on a white shirt with a blue sweater and blue jeans. When I come in the room, he doesn't fall on the floor because he's dumbstruck by how great I look. But he looks relieved to see me. That's better than nothing.

"The movie starts in a few minutes," he says to Mom and Joe. "I guess we'd better be leaving."

He shakes their hands. Mom asks when we'll be back and Ben says about eleven, if that's okay. He opens the front door for me. I hope Mom notices that. She's always complaining if people don't have good manners. She practically gets catatonic if people don't say please or thank you all the time.

Ben's father is sitting in the car. He looks a lot like Ben, with green eyes and curly hair, but it's turned gray. I wonder if this is what Ben will look like in thirty years. That wouldn't be too bad. Mr. Cooper is cute in a very mature way. He reaches across the seat and shakes my hand. "I'm glad to finally meet you, Sarah."

Ben and I sit in the backseat together. There's about a foot and a half between the two of us. I guess we're supposed to make conversation right now. I don't know what to say, of course, even though I spent the past three hours looking at dating tips in some of the magazines I've got. They all say the same thing. *Be a good listener.* But that's hard if nobody else is talking. They also say to be yourself. But what if you're a big washout like me? I don't want to be myself. Why should I? I've been myself all my life. I want to be somebody better for a change. Especially tonight.

"How do you two know each other?" Mr. Cooper asks.

Great. I don't know much about dating, but I do

know that the parents aren't supposed to talk more than the kids. I bet Ben is already wishing he was at home watching reruns on TV. I'm probably more boring than a laugh track.

"We have world history together," I say. "The class Coach Morrison used to teach. He's the guy who got fired for losing all those football games."

Last week we got a new world history teacher, Mr. Hutton, who's just out of college. He has a little mustache and a very good sense of humor. He told our class he hates football, and he wouldn't even know which way to run if he got the ball. Alex Baxter said, well, neither did Coach Morrison. That made everybody on the football team laugh.

Ben turns to me and grins. "It's amazing to have a teacher who knows something about history. Coach got surprised every year when he found out the South didn't win the Civil War. The suspense just about finished him off."

He and I start to laugh together. For the first time in days, I almost relax. Maybe we can be friends after all, I think. I glance down at his hands and wish I had the nerve to brush against them.

Mr. Cooper drops us off at the movie theater. Ashley Skiles is there in the lobby with Sam and a bunch of other popular people. They look like they have a spotlight shining on them so everybody will see how gorgeous they are and how much fun they're having. Ashley swings her hair back and forth over her shoulders, from one side to the other, like she's doing calisthenics with her hair. Doing something like that can get you lots of back problems when you're older. Ashley may become a hunchback someday if she doesn't cut it out.

But for once, I don't envy Ashley the way I usually do. I'd rather be here with Ben than with anybody on earth. We stand in the refreshment line together, talking a little, and I feel so happy that I should probably go ahead and die right now. Ben gets a jumbo popcorn and two soft drinks, but I don't think I can eat anything. I haven't been hungry for days, not even for junk food.

The movie we see is a comedy that isn't very funny. It's about a guy who wins the lottery, so he quits his job and leaves his wife and children. Then he realizes he's unhappy, so he starts giving away all his money. By the time his money is gone, he's a lot happier and he's fallen back in love with his wife and they're about to get remarried. I don't think it's very realistic. Also, it's extremely sexist. The guy's wife is supposed to be waiting around for him to wise up and come back to his family. They always make women wait around in these movies. I don't think waiting around for a man is a good idea, even though I'm kind of doing it right now with Ben. But I'm just a teenager. I'm supposed to do dumb things, aren't I? I plan on being a lot smarter when I'm a sophomore.

Halfway through the movie, Ben reaches over and holds my hand. It's wonderful. I feel like some kind of warm river has just splashed over me. It's even better than I expected. If sex feels this good, then I can hardly wait. I hope my palm doesn't start sweating, though. I glance at Ben and he turns toward me. I can see the lights from the movie on his face, like moving stripes painted across it. He grins and squeezes my hand. I feel wonderful.

The movie doesn't get much better, but I like it a lot more. Maybe it's okay to wait for someone just for a little while. Maybe the wife knew what she was doing. It's hard to tell, though. Everything in the movie is just about the guy and what a hard time he has and how he finally grows up in the end. It never shows the woman having any kind of life or thoughts or emotions. I think that's because almost all directors are men. That's what Mom always says, anyway.

But mostly I don't notice the movie. I just sit there in the dark with Ben. Even though there are about a million people around us, I feel like we're the only two people on earth. When the movie's over and the lights come back on, I'm disappointed. I want to sit there in the dark for the rest of my life. When you're this happy, you shouldn't have to go anywhere.

We walk outside, and Mr. Cooper is there waiting for us. He asks about the movie and we tell him about it. Ben says it was boring. I say it was very male dominated. Mr. Cooper laughs and asks if that means I'm a feminist. I say yes, I am.

"That must be hard at Hillside Park," Mr. Cooper says.

"I think it's important to think for yourself," I say.

The minute I say that, I feel pretty dumb. I'm not sure I even think for myself. I think I just like the idea of thinking for myself. Right now, I'd rather have more friends and not even think at all. I know that sounds terrible. But that's the way I feel. I wonder why HPHS is supposed to be such a good school if it's making me dumber like this. Or maybe it's hormones. I think hormones can make you dumb. Also, I may have more hormones than most people.

When we get to my house, Ben walks me up to my front door. The front-porch light is on. Mom must have put a thousand-watt bulb in it this time, because it's like the sun's come out and it's high noon or something. It's very embarrassing.

I look up at Ben. "I had a great time," I say.

He leans down and kisses me right on the lips. It

just lasts a second, but it's wonderful. I think it should count as foreplay. "Good night," he says, and walks off. When he gets a few steps away, he turns around and waves at me.

I go inside and peer out the peephole. I can see the Coopers' car moving silently along the street. I watch their lights get smaller and smaller till they disappear in the dark.

At first, when I get home, I'm still really excited. My heart's pounding about a million beats a minute. I keep reliving the kiss and holding hands with Ben, and it makes me feel like I'm floating in the clouds. I wish it wasn't so late. I'm dying to call Stephanie and tell her all about it.

But after a few minutes I start to get tired. I haven't slept much ever since Ben called me and all of a sudden I feel exhausted, like I've just run a marathon or something. I like dating a lot, but I think it's very tiring.

So I go to bed and fall asleep right away and I don't even think about anything or have any dreams till I hear the phone ringing. I look at my clock, and it's only 8 A.M., so I know it isn't Stephanie. She doesn't believe in calling people before noon. Mom must have gotten the phone, though. I can hear her talking downstairs. I roll over and pull a pillow over my head.

A few minutes later I hear a knock on my door. Mom comes in. Her face is tight and sad. It looks like someone's pulling her skin back from her eyes and mouth.

She comes and sits on my bed and takes my hand. She has tears in her eyes. I watch a tear spill out and slide down her cheek. It just slips along and then falls off on her robe and makes a damp spot. I've never seen Mom cry before. I didn't think she could.

"Mom, what's—"

"It's Madeleine." She squeezes my hand and looks me directly in the eye. "Oh, Sarah, Ellie just called. Madeleine killed herself last night."

sixteen

When Ellie and I were younger, we used to talk about dying a lot. I'm not sure why. Maybe it's because we were always writing letters about people on death row. I guess we thought about death a lot more than other kids our age.

Sometimes we'd tell each other what we wanted when we died. We both wanted to be cremated, because we hated the idea of being buried. Ellie wanted to have a really small service at her home. She said she didn't like the idea of being in a church because she didn't think that churches served social justice. She didn't want lots of flowers around, either. Ellie thought that flowers were a big waste of money. She wanted everything to be very quiet and simple.

That's all I can think about while I'm at Madeleine's funeral. I wonder what Madeleine would have wanted her funeral to be like. I wonder if anyone knows what she wanted. I don't. I didn't even know Madeleine that well, even though I'd been at her house off and on for the past three years. I don't think anyone knew Madeleine that well.

The funeral's in the chapel at Hillside Park Presbyterian Church, and I'm sitting in the third row with Mom and Joe, right behind Ellie's family. The altar has flowers everywhere—white and pink carnations and red poinsettias and even some green holly with red berries. Flowers are all I can smell. They're heavy and too sweet, and they're starting to make me sick. I can't breathe air like this.

The organ is droning on and on, too. I don't know what the name of the hymn is, but it's as heavy and sad and sweet as the flowers. It drags on and on and on, and I think I'm going to pass out if it doesn't stop soon.

Madeleine's casket is white, and it sits in the middle of all the flowers. It's small and thin and everything else is so much bigger. Her casket is like a tiny white toothpick in the middle of all that color. If they weren't going to cremate her, I wish they'd at least put her in a bigger casket so she wouldn't seem so crushed by all of this—the smell, the music, the flowers, all the people, all the noise, everything. Even though the organ's loud, I can hear people crying over it.

Mrs. Peterson is leaning over her handkerchief. She has her arm around Ellie and they're both crying harder than I've ever heard anyone cry before. Mr.

Peterson and Misty are right behind them. He's staring straight ahead and he's so still it's as if he were carved out of a mountain. Misty's crying, though. Every few minutes I can see her shoulders shake and she leans against Mr. Peterson. He doesn't seem to notice. He just stares ahead, like nobody else is in the chapel.

Ellie's two grandmothers are in the same row as Mr. Peterson and Misty. I've only seen pictures of them before. I don't think they were very close to Madeleine, since no one ever talked about them. There was also a woman and two men in that row, and I guess they must be an aunt and uncles.

"Let us pray."

The minister's up there, dressed in a long white robe. That's the way the minister was dressed at Dad's funeral. They must think it looks more cheerful than wearing black.

"Dear God, we come to you to ask for your help today. We know so little . . . and you know so much. We ask your blessings and your love to be with us while we mourn the death of this beautiful young woman . . . and pray for her to have eternal life at your side. In Christ's name we ask. Amen."

After that we stand and sing a hymn called "How Great Thou Art." I wonder if Madeleine liked this hymn. I doubt it. I never heard her mention liking any kind of religious music. Madeleine really was nonverbal most of the time. She did like the kind of music where the band sounds like it's screaming and bashing its guitars against the wall and vomiting very loudly. I know that because I used to hear her play that music in her room. But I don't think they play music like that in church even if you request it.

"Will you please be seated?"

It's that minister again. I saw him yesterday at the Petersons' house. He looked very sad, as if he knew Madeleine personally. I don't think he did, though. I think the Petersons had just gone to his church for a few weeks. I think that joining the church had something to do with Mrs. Peterson's real estate career.

"This is Sarah," Mrs. Peterson said to the minister. She pulled me into some kind of hug. I felt like I was being strangled, but I didn't want to move. "Sarah is a very close friend of our family, and Madeleine always looked up to her. Sarah, this is Dr. Parker."

Dr. Parker took my hand and looked me straight in the eyes and told me he knew how hard it must be for me to get through this. He had tears in his eyes, but I didn't. I didn't cry when I heard Madeleine had killed herself. I didn't cry yesterday, when I was at her house. And I'm not crying today, when I'm at her funeral. I'm one of these people who cries about ten times a day, but I can't right now. I don't know why. I'm just looking around, noticing things, and my eyes are dry and my heart feels like a concrete block. This is the way I was at Dad's funeral, too. I used to think I was a very emotional person, but maybe I'm wrong. Maybe I don't have any real emotions at all.

Even when I saw Ellie yesterday, I didn't cry. I couldn't think of much to say, either. I told her I was sorry. That was the only thing I could think of.

If you saw her from a distance Ellie looked pretty much the same. But the closer I got to her, the more I realized she was different. Her eyes had changed. I can't explain how, exactly, except they looked empty and dead. There were people coming up to her and hugging her and telling her how sorry they were about her loss. There was all of that. But even though she was surrounded by people, Ellie looked so sad and alone that I wanted to die for her. I couldn't, though. All I could say was how sorry I was, too. That didn't mean anything. That's what everyone was saying. If I'd been her best friend, if I'd been as good a friend to her as she was to me, I would have been there with her. But I wasn't. And I knew I couldn't go back to that even if I wanted to. I don't know how I knew that, but I did.

Right now Dr. Parker is standing at the front of the church, behind the pulpit. He says lots of things and sometimes I hear him and sometimes I don't. I feel like I'm about to choke every time I try to breathe. I feel like somebody has put his hands around my neck and started to squeeze. I let my head fall down and I try to relax.

Dr. Parker is saying how hard it is to lose someone as young and talented as Madeleine was. He says that a death like this is so difficult that it may make us question God's love for us and his plan for the world.

"We can grieve," he's saying, "and we should grieve. We've suffered a tremendous loss. But we can't give in to despair. Despair makes a mockery of God's world and his love for us. We can grieve—but we must continue to have faith."

He talks a little about Madeleine and what a good student she was. She loved her parents and her sister and her brother. She was a joy to be around. She cared about others much more than she cared about herself. Mrs. Peterson cries harder when he says that.

Dr. Parker talks on and on, but he doesn't say anything about Madeleine killing herself. He doesn't talk about how sad she was or how lonely. The more he talks, the more I realize he didn't know her at all. Maybe no one did. Is this how it all works? Maybe the minute someone dies, you get to change everything about that person. Anything you didn't like can disappear. Now that the person's gone, you get to draw the picture that you like.

I look down at my lap. There's a photograph of Madeleine on the front of the program. It's an oval, black-and-white photo, and she looks beautiful in it. Madeleine was never that beautiful. It hardly looks like her. I never saw her smile like that, either—a big, open smile that looks like she was delighted with the world and happy to be alive. She wasn't like that. She was someone else. I'm not sure who she was, but she wasn't that person. I don't think anybody knew who she was—so now they're trying to make her up.

Parents always say that when teenagers commit suicide, it's because they don't understand that death is permanent. They're simply feeling bad and they want to feel better. They don't realize what they're doing. I've read that a million times in magazines and newspapers and I think it's supposed to make parents feel better. But I don't think it's true. I think it's a lie.

I don't know much about Madeleine. But I do know that what the Petersons are saying right now is wrong. Yesterday at their house Mrs. Peterson went around saying that her former therapist Margaret had told her that Madeleine had just wanted to attempt suicide. Slashing her wrists and getting into a tub full of hot water had been a cry for help, Margaret had said. Madeleine had wanted to be found. She hadn't wanted to die. She loved her family too much to hurt them this way.

I got sick to my stomach when I heard that, because I knew it wasn't even close to the truth. I didn't know who they were talking about, but it wasn't Madeleine. They were talking about someone else. I think Madeleine slashed her wrists because she wanted to be dead. She wanted to leave this world and never come back. But no one wants to say that. They all want to pretend she didn't know what she was doing. *You know you don't mean that*—that's what the Petersons always say. That's what people always say about their kids.

I squeeze my eyes shut till they hurt. Everything inside me feels black and frozen and bitter. Ever since I heard that Madeleine killed herself, all I can think about is how sad and alone Ellie must be. It makes me feel terrible.

I remember all the times Ellie called me or left messages or tried to talk to me in the hall. I didn't want to hurt her or abandon her—but I knew I had. I knew I'd failed her terribly.

Ellie had been a good friend, a wonderful friend to me when I needed her the most, after Dad died. And what did I do for her? Not a damned thing. Not a goddamned thing. I was so selfish and self-absorbed and all I cared about was being in love with Ben and having other friends who were more fun than Ellie. When she needed me, I wasn't there. I didn't want to be there. She knew that. We both knew that. When her mother grabbed her and cried and held on till she strangled her. When her father was so busy with his new family. When her sister killed herself. That's why Ellie got so angry at me that night at her house—because I wasn't her friend any longer.

Ellie is all alone now. That's all I really know. And that's my fault. She must feel like she doesn't have any friends at all. I'll hate myself till the day I die for not being there for her when she needed me. I'll never forget it. How could I? Just being around her, I felt like a fraud. Everyone was still introducing me as a good friend of the family's. But I wasn't. I hadn't been a good friend to anyone but myself.

I turn the program over. At the very bottom, it says that Madeleine's family would like any memorial contributions to go to the building fund at Hillside Park Middle School. There's nothing about anything that meant anything to Madeleine while she was alive. No one had any idea what she would have wanted.

The day after Madeleine's funeral, the newspaper has a big story on its metro page about preteen suicides. It talks about Madeleine, but it doesn't mention her name. She's referred to as a twelve-year-old seventh grader at Hillside Park Middle School whose death "stunned" her friends and family.

"She was never any trouble to us—never. We had no warning at all"—that's the quote they used from Mrs. Peterson. The article calls her "the dead preteen's grief-stricken mother, who is thirty-three." When I see that, I realize that Mrs. Peterson is probably going to be all right. If she was extremely depressed, she wouldn't have remembered to subtract a few years off her age.

The article says that suicides are a growing problem among preteens nationwide—especially in affluent communities like Hillside Park. Often one preteen suicide can spark other young people's attempts to kill themselves, too, one psychiatrist says in the article. He gives a whole list of warning signs for parents to look for: lack of sleep, weight gain or loss, giving away possessions, changes in personality, loss of interest in the world. I can see all the parents in Hillside Park clipping that article and putting it on their Sub-Zero refrigerators and trying to figure out if their kids are about to kill themselves. Nana's been writing letters to Mom again, and I'm pretty sure she'll send a copy of this, marked with a lot of yellow highlighter.

Tuesday afternoon I go back to school. Ellie's not back yet. But everything else seems the same. Except that lots of people are talking about Ellie's sister committing suicide. I hear someone say that Ellie is kind of strange, too, just like her sister. I turn around when I hear that, but I can't tell who said it.

Stephanie told me that the school had an assembly in the gym about grief on Monday. Ms. Heath, the principal, spoke about how important it was for everyone to acknowledge their feelings of grief about a young person's death and not to suffer silently. "We all need each other at a time like this," she said. Stephanie swore up and down that Ashley Skiles cried during the whole assembly, even though it ruined her eye makeup. At first she thought it was because Ashley felt bad about Madeleine's death. But later she heard that Ashley was upset because she found out she has herpes.

"You used to be really good friends with her sister, didn't you?" Stephanie asks.

"Yeah," I say. "We were best friends for a long time."

We're sitting in the school cafeteria, eating lunch. It's loud, as usual. Everybody's screaming and laughing, and it's hard to talk or hear anything. But I want to say something more.

"Ellie is a very good person," I say. "But I didn't know Madeleine very well. I don't think anyone did."

I know Stephanie can tell I've said something, but I'm not sure if she can even hear what I'm saying. She nods and smiles at me. The noise gets even worse in the cafeteria, and for the rest of our lunchtime we don't even try to talk.

This week there are more stories in the newspaper and on the TV news about preteen suicide. I hear someone in the halls say it reminds them of the movie *Heathers* when everyone's waiting around for another kid to kill himself. One of the articles says that Madeleine's death may have been related to the kind of music she played. The headline says: *Suicidal Preteen Loved Bizarre Music.* The subhead says: *Psychologists Say Music Can Sway the Young into Danger.* There's a quote from Stephanie's father in it. He says that lots of teenagers like bizarre music, but that doesn't mean they're going to kill themselves. "Our parents used to think the Beatles were bizarre," he says. "Remember?"

Lots of rumors are also going around about how Madeleine's suicide may have been some kind of satanic ritual. "She was definitely a member of a cult," someone says one day in the bathroom. "And also that girls' gang. You know, the Chihuahuas." It's exactly like the time I heard that remark in the halls. By the time I look out, I can't tell who said that. It's just a row of girls. They're all looking in the mirror, putting on lipstick.

One afternoon when I leave school, there are two white news vans with station names all over them.

Two tall blond women, who look almost like twins even though they are from different stations, are standing there with microphones. I know one of them, since she works at the same station Mom does. I don't want her to see me and I don't want to talk to anyone, so I duck back inside the school and leave by another exit. Then I walk home as slowly as I can.

Ben called me last night, and we talked for fifty-three minutes this time. The second I heard his voice, I felt my stomach drop, like I was in an elevator. I thought that maybe I was too upset about Madeleine and Ellie to still be in love with Ben, but I guess I'm not. That makes me feel the way Ellie sometimes makes me feel. I feel shallow, like I'm not nearly as good a person as she is. When someone dies, you should think about only that person for a long, long time and your life should almost stop. That's the way it should be, isn't it? That's the way it was for me when Dad died. Everything stopped for a long, long time. But Madeleine's death hasn't stopped anything. And that makes me feel awful. I haven't even called Ellie. Maybe I should, but I don't want to. I know she'd realize I was calling her because I feel sorry for her. And not because we're friends any longer. We'd both know that.

I turn the TV on. There's a special news report about Bonnie Shepherd. Her petition to a state board has been turned down. The governor of Texas can delay her execution by thirty days if he wants. But he probably won't, the commentator says. It's another one of those blond women from TV. She's dressed in a black coat with a red scarf around her neck, and the wind is blowing the scarf behind her back. She's standing in a street across from the courthouse in Huntsville. That's the town in East Texas where they execute people.

"The crowds and the emotions are incredible tonight," the woman says. Around her you can see people with signs, jumping up and down and screaming. One woman is kneeling to pray, holding her little boy's hand. Another man moves his hand-lettered sign back and forth. *Fry in Hell for Your Sins, Bonnie Shepherd,* it says. For a few seconds the camera focuses on him and his sign. The man grins for the camera, and his eyes look bright and hard, like he's just won something.

"If we don't hear from the governor," the newswoman says, "Bonnie Shepherd will be executed in"—she looks at her watch—"in just over an hour." She signs off the air, and the two anchors say they'll bring us any breaking news about Bonnie Shepherd and her appeals to live. Behind them there's the newsreel of Bonnie Shepherd in her orange prison jumpsuit, walking in handcuffs, her long ponytail swinging back and forth.

"You're so quiet, Sarah," Mom says later that night. She just got home from work and we're eating dinner by ourselves in the kitchen. "Are you all right? Have you been thinking about Madeleine a lot?"

I shut my eyes. I wish Mom would leave me alone. I don't want to talk about Madeleine. I don't want to talk about Ellie, either. Right now I don't want to talk about anything.

"Are you feeling guilty about it?" Mom asks.

"What do you mean? Why should I feel guilty?"

Mom shrugs slightly. "I mean that you and Ellie were best friends for years. She spent a lot of time here and you spent a lot of time at her house. You might be feeling there was something you could have done—to help her and Madeleine. But there's no way you could have known what would happen. It wasn't your fault."

I get up from the table. For the first time in my life I scream at Mom. "No, goddammit! Of course it wasn't my fault! How can you even say that? How can you even think that?"

She and I stare at each other for a few seconds. "Sarah, I didn't mean—," she says.

"I don't care what you mean! Why don't you just shut up and leave me alone?"

I drop my napkin on the table and run upstairs to my room. I slam the door and throw myself on my bed so hard that it jolts me. I'm sick of everyone, especially Mom and all her dopey psychobabble questions. I want to forget everything. I want to be unconscious. I want to be somewhere far away. I don't want to be here. I don't want to be anywhere.

For the first time in days, I start to cry. I hold my pillow so tightly that it's crammed against my face. My whole body is shaking. I scream and I cry and I almost gag. Then I lie still and I feel empty. Then I start to cry again with huge, gasping sobs. I feel like I'm shaking the house, I'm crying so hard. But for a long time I can't stop.

I'm crying for myself and Madeleine and Ellie. And Dad and Mom. I'm crying for Nana, even if she doesn't deserve it. And Bonnie Shepherd, even though she's a murderer. I'm crying because life is so damned sad and I can't figure out why we're all so terrible to each other. I want to think that we can be good and love each other. But we can't, can we? We keep hurting each other over and over, making our lives worse. Why can't we do better than this? Why can't I do better than this?

I cry because I hate myself for everything I've done to Ellie and because I didn't even know Madeleine. I cry because everything's so sad and useless, and I don't even know why we keep trying. It never gets us anywhere, does it? It only hurts us more. I cry until I'm so tired I can't even get up to change my clothes. I just fall asleep there, on top of my bed. It's so dark I can't even see myself.

The next afternoon I walk to Ellie's house after school. She hasn't come back to school yet. I heard she won't be back till next week.

Everything's quiet at the Petersons' house for once. I ring the doorbell, but I can't hear anything. No one answers, so I ring it again. I'm about to leave when the door opens. It's Ellie. She stands there, blinking in the sunlight. Behind her the house is dark.

Ellie looks so sad and lonely that I want to hug her. Her eyes are red and her face is paler than it used to be. I try to look into her eyes, but it's hard. Her eyes are empty and dull, the way they were at the funeral. I remember what her eyes used to look like, when she was excited about the letters we were writing and how they could help other people. She was so full of life then, and now she doesn't seem to have any life left.

I want to cry, because she looks so sad and hopeless. I want to do something for her. I want to take all her sadness and feel it for a few days so she can rest. Can I do that? Can I just reach out and take it on so she'll be all right and she won't have to hurt all the time? Of course I can't. I know that. It's impossible. But God, I want to so badly.

"I just want to tell you how sorry I am," I say.

That's all I can say, but I want to say so much more. I want to tell her how sorry I am about Madeleine's death and about not being a good and loyal friend to her. I want to tell her how much I appreciated her being a friend to me when I needed her so much after Dad died. I want to tell her how terrible I feel that I wasn't that same kind of friend to her. I want to tell her that my heart is breaking for her and I don't know what to do. But I'd do something, anything, to make her life better if I could. I would.

I think all of this. But something in me knows that it's too late. Sometimes you turn around, and everything behind you is gone. You have to go somewhere else.

"Ellie—I—" I don't even know what I'm trying to say. I don't want to cry or say anything more. I just want Ellie to understand how sorry I am. That's all I can do now. That's all I have left.

I hold out my hand and Ellie takes it. For a minute we just look at each other. We're both crying, with tears spilling down our cheeks. But we don't say anything. And we don't move any closer to each other.

I look in Ellie's eyes and see they aren't empty any

longer. There's something in them that touches me, something I can almost feel. It's understanding, I realize slowly. It's understanding, and it's something else I haven't seen too often in my life. It's some kind of forgiveness. She knows what I did, but she forgives me anyway. I don't deserve it, but she's giving it to me. I want to help her, but she's helping me instead.

Ellie and I hug each other. For a few minutes we stand there and cry together. Then she draws back. She stands straighter, like she's trying to look strong.

"I've got to go now," she says.

Ellie steps back inside her house and closes the door quietly. I turn around and walk home. Somehow I know I'll never go back and I know Ellie knows that, too.

I still feel sad and I brush tears away while I walk. But I feel better, too. For the first time in days, I feel almost peaceful.

17 seventeen

After Christmas, Mom and I go skiing. She's taking a week off from work for the first time I can remember. Joe's not going with us, though. Mom says that he's too busy this time of year. Besides, she thinks it's good for the two of us to get away together. That's nice of her, I guess. She knows I've always wanted to go skiing. But I'm not sure what we're going to talk about for a week. Maybe I should have brought lots of books with me.

We leave from the airport at night. I'm sitting by the window and I look out and watch the ground get farther and farther away. All the lights from the city look like jewels and the darkness is like some kind of black velvet. I think I'll write that sentence down before I forget it. It would be a good description to use in an English paper. Ms. Evans says she expects us to write something creative about what we did over the holiday break.

Maybe the plane will crash. That would help me write an extremely creative paper. I could also write an article about the plane crash for the school newspaper. Headline: *HPHS Freshman Wins Pulitzer Prize for First-Person Account of Fiery DFW Crash;* subhead: *"Anyone Could Have Done It," Says Modest Student.*

The plane bumps up and down, and everyone laughs very nervously. I hate that. Maybe I don't want the plane to crash after all. If it started going down, I'm pretty sure I'd be screaming bloody murder. I might even lose control of my bladder or something. Then I'd probably push in front of everybody else, trying to get to the exit. I'm not a very heroic person. I'd be better off writing a third-person account of a plane crash.

"God, I hate turbulence," Mom says. "I don't want to die in a crowd like this. I don't like the looks of anybody." Her jaws are clenched. She motions to the flight attendant to bring her a drink. "A double bourbon on the rocks."

The plane settles down and flies more smoothly. Mom stirs her drink and sips it carefully. She hates turbulence and so do I. I never realized that before. Dad was different. Dad loved turbulence. He said that otherwise, flying in a big plane was too damned boring. A little turbulence made things interesting. A lot of turbulence made things fascinating. That's what he always said. It was true for him, I guess.

To be honest, I don't like flying that much. But I'm

glad to get out of town right now. I want to get away and never go back. Maybe if I get farther away, I can think more clearly. I hope so, anyway.

Mom and Joe and I spent Christmas together and it was okay. But it was hard to feel excited about Christmas the way I used to. I always thought that I'd get a present that would change my life and make everything better. So every year I'd look forward to Christmas and every year I'd be disappointed. I'm not like that any longer. Maybe that's better. I don't get disappointed as much as I used to. I don't know if that's good or not.

Joe proposed to Mom on Christmas Eve. I knew he was going to do it, because he told me about it the week before. He took me out one afternoon so we could look for diamond rings. He had me try them on, since Mom's hands and mine are exactly the same size. I've never been around so many jewels in my life. It was fun. Joe was nervous the whole time. He kept running his fingers over his bald spot and chewing gum. He sounded like the rhythm section in our school band.

"Which one do you think your mother would like best?" he kept asking me. "You know her taste better than anyone, Sarah. Men don't know anything about jewelry. We're completely helpless at times like this."

He slipped me two pieces of gum across the counter.

"This will help you think. Gum always helps me think better."

I put the gum in my mouth and chewed it slowly. "Have you decided?" Joe asked. "Or do you need more gum?"

The ring he finally bought Mom was platinum with a round diamond in it. I'm not sure what it cost, but it must have been a lot, because Joe kept making jokes about taking out a second mortgage on his condo. He didn't seem to mind, though. He looked very happy.

"I'm forty-four," he said while the clerk was wrapping the ring. "Forty-four. But I'd never been in love with anyone before I met your mother." He drummed his fingers on the counter and frowned. "Well, I guess I've been infatuated a few times. But not in love. Love's different. You'll find that out someday, Sarah."

When Mom opened the package, she started to cry. That was the second time I've ever seen her cry. These days she's practically crying more than I am. When I saw her cry, I almost cried, too. Even Joe had tears in his eyes. It was very romantic. If I ever get engaged, I hope the ring is so pretty and I'm so happy that I start bawling just like that. It would be a nice memory to have, kind of like a good movie.

After that we had Christmas dinner and Nana came over. She hadn't been to our house in ages, so it was a very big deal. Mom refused to go to Nana's house. She said she was tired of Nana hogging all the holidays.

The first time she said that, Nana hung up on her. Nana's hanging up on a lot of people these days. One time she told me it was much more ladylike to hang up on people than to scream at them. But anyway, she called Mom back after about half an hour and pretended her phone had gotten disconnected. She said she'd love to have Christmas dinner with us, as long as Mom didn't try to show off and make something fancy. She said that turkey was good enough for the Wise Men, and it was good enough for us, too. Mom said that was all right with her. She was tired of cooking complicated recipes, anyway.

The whole time she was at our house, Nana was on pretty good behavior. "This turkey is more than adequate, Dinah," she said. "More than adequate. The mashed potatoes are a little lumpy, though."

She dabbed at her mouth with a cloth napkin and smiled at Mom and Joe and me. Mom hadn't told her anything about being engaged to Joe. She didn't like to tell Nana about anything important. She said she guessed she'd have to invite Nana to the wedding, though.

After the plates were cleared, Nana got very sentimental and started talking about how all her friends were dead. She said she wondered how much time she had left, too. This time she was dabbing at her eyes with a handkerchief, even though I couldn't see any tears in her eyes. Nana's always dabbing at something. It's one of her nervous habits.

"I hope I'll be able to carry on by myself," she said. She spilled some coffee on the carpet, but she didn't notice it. "Otherwise I may have to move in with you and Sarah, Dinah."

Mom's face looked exactly the way it had when Misty had told her she had flabby arms. Fortunately the door-bell rang then. It was Ben. He wanted to see if I could go on a walk with him, since it was so warm today.

That's how Ben ended up meeting Nana. The moment she saw him, she forgot all about moving in with us. She spent all her time asking Ben who his father was and what he did for a living.

"Cooper? I don't know any Coopers. Has your family lived here long?"

By the time I was able to drag Ben away, Nana had decided she might know Ben's aunt through her church. Also, she said that one of her friends who just died, Lucille Tompkins, might have known one of his grandmothers in the best rest home in town.

"Lucille was one of those friends I'll never replace," Nana said. She was dabbing at her eyes again. "She and I went to Vassar together, you know."

Ben said no, he didn't know that. Then I pulled him

outside and we went for a walk. Even though it was winter, it was warm and sunny. If the trees hadn't been so bare, you wouldn't have known it was winter. It felt like springtime.

We walked to the park and fed the ducks. Then we sat on a bench and watched the breeze blow the water in the creek bed. Ben put his arm around me and I leaned against him, just a little. I felt warm and happy. Maybe I'd been wrong about Christmases not being so great once you got older.

After about an hour we walked back to my house. Nana was already gone, and Mom and Joe were cleaning up the kitchen.

"Your grandmother offered to send her maid over to help," Mom said. I asked Mom if she meant Josefina, and Mom said no, Josefina had already quit three weeks ago. Since then, Nana had gone through three more maids. Also, she was trying to have Josefina deported, but she couldn't remember what country she came from.

"Is Nana moving in with us?" I asked.

"Over my dead body," Mom said.

She turned and looked at me, and we both smiled.

I sleep on the plane till we land in Boston. We spend about half an hour in line before we can rent a car, then Mom and I stay in a Boston hotel for the night. The next morning we get up early and drive to Vermont.

I've been to New England once or twice before, but I've never been here in the winter. It's beautiful. There's snow everywhere along the roads and in the forests and fields and on the tops of roofs, and the trees are bare and dark.

Today it's clear, but tomorrow it's supposed to snow more. There might even be a blizzard. I hope so. I've never seen a blizzard in my life. I've always wanted to be snowed in somewhere. I think that would be very romantic. It wouldn't be very romantic to get snowed in with your mother, though, and have your boyfriend a thousand miles away. *My boyfriend.* That's what I call Ben sometimes. Just to myself, of course. I wouldn't want anyone to hear me say that. But I've practiced it a lot and I really like the way it sounds.

It's early afternoon by the time we finally get to the ski resort. Everywhere I look, there are mountains and piles of pure white snow and tiny figures in bright outfits. This is the most exciting place I've ever been to in my life.

After we put our bags in our room, Mom and I get dressed in ski clothes. We both have winter underwear and pants and sweaters and parkas. I borrowed mine from Stephanie, which is why they're sort of baggy. Stephanie's legs are about nine inches longer than mine.

For the next two hours we take a private lesson from an instructor named Josee. She's French Canadian, and she has all her strawberry blond hair scooped up into a ponytail. She's also very cheerful.

"My theory is—everyone can learn to ski," she says, beaming at us. "It doesn't matter how old you are."

Josee teaches Mom and me how to snowplow to stop or slow down. It feels weird at first—leaning forward when I want to lean back. But the more I practice it, the easier it is. Even the skis don't feel as heavy and awkward as they did at first. I slip down the hill slowly at first. Then I pick up a little more speed. When I go faster, it's so easy that it feels like flying.

"I like this!" I tell Mom.

She's lying on the ground in a heap. It must be the fiftieth time she's fallen. One ski's off, lying in the snow, and the other's sticking up in the air.

"I hate it," she says.

Josee helps her up and dusts some of the snow off Mom's red parka. "Try to be patient," she says. "You're making good progress."

Mom sighs loudly. She slides a little bit, then she falls down again. "That sound you heard is my ego cracking," she says. "I think I'll stay here for a while."

Josee smiles uncertainly. She's one of these people who's too serious to get Mom's humor, especially since it's not in French. So she skis along with me, and after a few minutes she's beaming again.

"I think you are both ready to take the lift up the hill," she says happily. She doesn't notice that Mom is crossing her eyes when she says that. "Then we'll go down the beginners' slope together."

Mom says she doesn't want to go on the ski lift just yet.

"You two go on," she says. "I feel much more confident falling at the bottom of the mountain."

Josee looks confused.

"I mean it," Mom says.

Josee and I catch the ski lift and go up the mountain. I turn around and watch Mom get smaller and smaller. She's not watching us, though. She's not doing anything. She's just lying in the snow with her arms out to the side. She's a small red streak on the white hill. When we turn a corner, I can't see her any longer.

We jump off at the top, and Josee holds on to my arm so I won't fall. It's not that hard, really. We ski jerkily down the paths and I fall once or twice when I get going faster. Even when I fall, I don't mind. There's nobody here I know, so I don't feel self-conscious. When I can stay upright and move from side to side, something about it feels wonderful. I feel free and happy. I've never been athletic, ever, but I like this.

When we get to the bottom, Mom's sitting up in the snow and she looks extremely cross. Josee says she'll stay with her. I wave at both of them and jump on the ski lift again.

It's strange. I can't remember ever seeing Mom do so badly at something. She's always been good at everything—work, talking, writing, anything she ever tried. It's funny, too, for me to be better at something than Mom is. The truth is, I like it.

I ride to the top of the mountain again and again and follow the trails down the side of the mountain till the sky starts to get dark. The last time I'm at the top, I take off my skis and walk around for a few minutes. Everywhere I can see, it's white and pure and beautiful, stretching from mountain to mountain, till it all gets lost in the winter sky. It's the most beautiful place I've ever been and it makes me feel good. While I'm here, I can forget everything.

I breathe in the cold air and start down the mountain again. Even for a few minutes, it's good to feel so free and happy.

After dinner Mom and I sit in front of the fireplace in our room. I feel sore and tired, but I can hardly wait to get up in the morning and go skiing again.

"That's fine," Mom says, making a face. "Just don't wake me up. I'm taking a vacation from our vacation."

The fire crackles, and she nudges it with a small branch. Her hair falls into her face and she brushes it back impatiently. As usual, it falls into place perfectly.

Right now Mom looks the way she always has—confident and poised and pretty and all those things I want to be, but I'm not. But for once, I'm seeing her a little differently. First, I saw her cry twice. Then, I saw her fall down again and again today. I was never dumb enough to think Mom was perfect or anything. But I used to think she was so much tougher than I am that I never saw how we could be related. It's nice to see that that's not all she is.

"Today was funny," I say. "I've never seen you when you weren't good at something."

Mom looks at me, then she looks back at the fire. She smiles. "I've never felt I was that good at anything. But the older you get, the better you get at pretending. It's compensation for wrinkles and varicose veins."

Something about what she's saying squeezes my heart and, for a minute, I want to cry. But I don't. I just tell her what I've been thinking for the past few hours. "I'm glad we made this trip. It means a lot to me."

"I know," Mom says. She pats me on the arm. "I've

thought about that. This is the trip you were going to make with your father."

She pokes at the fire again. "Do you think of him much?"

I shake my head. "I try not to think of him. Sometimes I feel like I hate him." I take a deep breath and the words start pouring out faster. "I feel like I spent most of my life worshiping him. Then he died and I found out who he really was. I loved him, but he wasn't who I thought he was. His drinking ... his driving ... well, he practically killed himself the way Madeleine did. When I heard he'd taken money from Aunt Dottie's estate, I wanted to die.

"I don't know who Dad was anymore. I don't even know if he loved me, really—or if I still love him."

It's quiet in the room for a few minutes. Mom and I sit there, side by side, without looking at each other. We both stare straight ahead into the fire.

"I want you to understand something, Sarah," Mom says. "I want you to listen to me for a minute. I know you're still young, but sometimes you have to grow up about things faster than you want to.

"Look at me." Mom turns and stares in my eyes. She has tears in hers. "You weren't wrong about your father. You're right—he wasn't a saint. He lived too hard and took too many risks and I guess you can talk about his shady financial dealings, if you want. I know he always meant to pay back Aunt Dottie's estate. He just got further and further behind and then he couldn't.

"That's true. That's all true. But it's not all of the truth. The truth is, your father was a good man and he loved you more than anyone else on earth. I know you're trying to understand everything else that he did ... the ways that he failed ... and that's all right. You have to do that. But you can't ever forget how much he loved you. You weren't wrong about that.

"And maybe that's what you have to decide in your own life. You have to decide if you're going to love him, too, no matter what he did. No matter how many mistakes he made. No matter how far he fell short of what you thought he was. Because that's how he loved you."

When I start to cry, she puts her arms around me and hugs me and pats me on the back. I guess that's the way most mothers act all the time. But Mom has never done that much to me. It's good just to cry and cry and have somebody pat me on the back and tell me everything's going to be all right.

And maybe it will be. You never know.

I spend the next day skiing while Mom sits in a sauna most of the time. She says she's much more talented at taking saunas than she is at skiing.

That night I wake up and look outside my window and everything's white. The weather forecasters said it was an honest-to-God blizzard. It's a blur outside my window, soft and white and peaceful. It's like seeing another world that I've never seen before.

I sit up and wrap a blanket around my knees and another blanket around my shoulders and watch the snow come down silently. I think about Ellie and Ben and Stephanie and Mom and Nana. I think about my whole life and how much it hurts sometimes. Mom talks about getting older and how, at least, you get smarter. I guess she's right. She hasn't told me how much more you hurt, the older you get. Maybe that's something you leave your kids to learn about on their own. Or maybe you hope they'll never have to figure that out. I don't know.

I think about all those people in my life. I think about the ways we all fail each other and hurt each other. But maybe that isn't the most important thing. Maybe the most important thing is that we go on trying. Do you think so? No matter how terrible we are or how much we fail, we go on trying, picking ourselves up, trying again. Reaching out. Trying again. Do you think that's true? Maybe it is. I'd like to think so.

I sit there and stare out the window. Finally I realize why I woke up in the first place. I'd been dreaming about Dad.

I could still see him in that dream, the way I always used to see him. His hands were outstretched and he was smiling a big, happy grin. I hadn't seen him in so long, and I'd missed him so much.

In my dream, I walked closer and closer to him. I didn't reach out and touch him. I just looked at him, as closely as I could. When I looked in his face, it was like it had always been. It was warm and happy and full of love.